the good girl

the good girl

Kerry Cohen Hoffmann

DELACORTE PRESS

Published by Delacorte Press
an imprint of Random House Children's Books
a division of Random House, Inc.
New York

Delacorte Press and colophon are registered trademarks
of Random House, Inc.

Visit us on the Web! www.randomhouse.com/teens
Educators and librarians, for a variety of teaching tools,
visit us at www.randomhouse.com/teachers

Library of Congress Cataloging-in-Publication Data
Hoffmann, Kerry Cohen.
The good girl / Kerry Cohen Hoffmann. — 1st ed.
p. cm.
Summary: After the death of her brother and the divorce of her parents,
overachieving high school sophomore Lindsey resorts to petty thievery as she
struggles under tremendous pressure to keep everything going smoothly at
home and at school.
ISBN 978-0-385-73644-2 (hardcover)
ISBN 978-0-385-90609-8 (hardcover lib. bdg.)
[1. Emotional problems—Fiction. 2. Stealing—Fiction. 3. Family problems—
Fiction. 4. Self-acceptance—Fiction. 5. Interpersonal relations—Fiction.
6. High schools—Fiction. 7. Schools—Fiction.] I. Title.
PZ7.H67546Go 2008   [Fic]—dc22   2008004686

The text of this book is set in 11.75-point Baskerville.
Book design by Vikki Sheatsley
Printed in the United States of America
10 9 8 7 6 5 4 3 2 1
First Edition

for all those who've felt they had to be
something for someone else

1

The first time I did it, I couldn't believe I was doing it. I was supposed to be getting my dad some aspirin from the hall bathroom. He knew I'd get it for him, too, because that was what I always did. I did the right thing, the nice thing. So when I took the twenty out of his wallet, which was sitting open on the console in the hallway, I was surprised. I was still surprised as I pocketed the money and returned the wallet to the table. I didn't breathe a word to Dad when I went into the kitchen, just poured him a glass of water and smiled as I let the pills fall into his open hand.

"Thank you," he said after he'd swallowed them. He nodded at me, like I was excused.

And I walked away, into my bedroom, where I took out the bill.

Look at that.

Later that evening, after I was supposed to be asleep, I started to feel nervous about taking the money. The apartment was quiet. Shadows from cars passing on the street below crept along the wall of my bedroom like little animals. Like the energy moving through my body, my eyes darting back and forth as I thought. Tomorrow Dad was leaving for an out-of-town meeting at 6 a.m. I knew

1

because I had made him a snack to take with him in the car. I'd set up his coffee, like I always did, to start brewing half an hour before he left. He would go to the drive-thru at Burger King or he would stop for more coffee at Starbucks. And he would open his wallet. And he'd see. For a split second, I wanted that, for him to see, for me to be caught. The anxiety pushed at my throat. My heart jumped around in my chest. Finally, I couldn't stand it anymore. I got up and tiptoed into the hallway. Tara's bedroom door was closed, and so was my dad's. The only open door was the one to Mark's room—the room that no one had touched, that had been full of taped-shut boxes, ever since Mark died. It was dark enough that I couldn't see anything, so I glided my hand along the wall, moving toward the table. But when I got there, the wallet was gone. And that was how it started. I'd done this thing, and there was no turning back.

And then I couldn't seem to stop.

2

Third period, before lunch, I was called into Ms. Keller's office. I went there slowly, trying to steady my breaths. I was certain I would see my father when I arrived. He would be frowning, disappointed. His precious reputation as the local psychiatrist tarnished. How could his good daughter fail him? So I was confused when my father was not in Ms. Keller's office, and instead there was a very cute boy with curly brown hair and a backpack. He nodded at me as I walked in, and then he smiled, and two dimples popped into his cheeks. I looked at Ms. Keller, my hands clasped behind my back.

"Lindsey." She came to stand beside me, her heels clicking. I liked Ms. Keller. She had been the headmaster of Bergen County Day when Mark had been here too, and she'd attended Mark's funeral. Ever since, we'd had an unspoken respect for each other, one based on the knowledge of my loss. Plus, Ms. Keller had made me sophomore ambassador this year, which meant I did special projects, and touring a new student was one of these. Being an ambassador was an honor. There was only one per grade, and Ms. Keller announced her picks at a school meeting at the end of each school year.

"Meet Kyle." She put a hand on my shoulder and faced the boy. "This is our best sophomore student," she told him.

Kyle looked right at me. His face was open and interested, so much so that I averted my eyes. "The best, huh?" he said, sounding amused.

"Kyle is from Vermont, and he's starting at BCD today," Ms. Keller said. "I'd like you to show him around."

I still couldn't look directly at him, so I stole glances instead. He just kept smiling.

"Follow me, I guess," I said.

And he did.

We walked down the hallway together. Everyone else was in class already, and it was very quiet. So quiet I could hear the swish of my jeans rubbing together as I walked. I cleared my throat, not wanting Kyle to hear too.

"What class are you in now?" I asked him.

"I thought you were supposed to know."

I stopped walking. "Maybe I should go back and ask Ms. Keller."

He laughed. It was a sweet, relaxed laugh. "No," he said. "Just show me around. I'll go to class later. I know my schedule."

I stayed still, uncomfortable. "But that's cutting."

He smiled again. "The best sophomore student."

Why did he have to keep saying that, like it was a bad thing? I looked at the door next to me. It was Mr. Little's biology classroom, where I'd be next period. Inside, Claire waved. She didn't see Kyle with me. I stepped quickly back so no one else would see us. "So?" I said, knowing I sounded defensive, and hating it.

4

"So you're one of those chicks who live by the rules," he said.

"First of all," I said, "I'm not a *chick*. Second of all, I see nothing wrong with doing the right thing." Of course, I couldn't help thinking about the fact that I had stolen money from my father the night before.

"It's lame," he said. "That's what's wrong with it. Sometimes you need to break the rules."

I started to say something about lame being relative, but he wasn't done.

"If you want to look back from your deathbed and see your main accomplishment as having done the right thing, that's your prerogative," he said. His face turned red and he crossed his arms. "It's not what *I* would want for *my* life."

Apparently this whole subject had hit a nerve.

We got silent then. Uncomfortably silent. I wished Ms. Keller had found someone else to escort this guy. I started walking, keeping my eyes straight ahead. I'm sure he wished Ms. Keller had found someone else too.

"This is the library," I said flatly when we reached the end of the hallway.

"Fascinating."

"You said you wanted me to show you around. That's what I'm doing."

"I don't want to see the building," he said, making me feel like the biggest idiot, no matter what my grades were. "Just show me the essentials. You know, like where my locker is and who I should avoid while I'm here."

I stared at him now. He really was cute, but he was obviously a jerk. I pointed down the stairs. "Your locker will be on the second floor," I said. I wasn't interested in being nice anymore.

"All righty, then." He walked ahead of me, confident, like he'd been here for years. Meanwhile, I was the one who'd been at BCD since seventh grade, and I still didn't feel confident. Not when people like Claire roamed the halls. Even though she was one of my best friends.

I followed him to the second floor and he pulled a folded paper from his pocket. He recited his locker number, and with a sinking feeling I led him to it.

"What are you doing?" he asked when I started opening the locker right next to his. My locker.

I looked up at him. "I'm who you should avoid while you're here."

"Hot-new-meat alert," Claire said as she approached me between periods. "Fresh from Vermont." Jo towered next to her, as usual. Missy, my very best friend, and I called Jo Claire's bobblehead because she was always nodding at everything Claire said. Jo was grinning wildly. Obviously, she thought Kyle was hot too.

"I know," I said. "Ms. Keller had me show him around."

"You?" Claire spit it out as if there was something wrong with me. Then she collected herself. She lifted a hand to smooth out her long blond hair. "Of course she picked you. You're BCD's star." She smiled big, but I was no fool. She hated that I'd gotten to meet Kyle before her.

"He's an asshole," I said to make her feel better.

"Really."

"Olivia Hanson says he's super-friendly," Jo said. Because Jo was so tall, she kept her head permanently cocked. This made her look like she was always empathizing, which was rarely the case. She was more interested in staying in Claire's good graces than anything else.

"Well, Olivia would say Hitler was super-friendly if she thought it would help her get in his pants," I told her.

Claire laughed. "So true," she said.

"Totally true," Jo agreed. She laughed along with Claire, and I made a point of not looking at her. It was simply too pathetic.

"Come with me," I told Claire. "I'll introduce you."

Claire's heavily made-up eyes widened. She looked at Jo, who widened her eyes back.

"Should I?"

"Of course you should," Jo said.

Claire pulled a compact from her purse and checked herself out. "My hair looks like crap today."

Jo deepened the angle of her head. She had red hair and so many freckles that they all sort of came together to make a few big freckles across her cheeks and nose. "No, it doesn't. You look great. You're the most beautiful girl in the tenth grade."

Claire smiled and snapped the compact closed. She and Jo had this exchange at least once a day. *Claire:* I'm not perfect in some way. *Jo:* You are *so* perfect. *Claire:* That's why I let you follow me around all day.

Sometimes I felt bad for Jo because boys never liked her, and here she was best friends with the girl every boy did like. But right now, she was just annoying me. Claire

7

wasn't just beautiful. She was also smart and could be lots of fun. In the past two years, there had been many times Claire had made me laugh so hard I almost peed in my pants. But when Jo was around, Claire became mean and arrogant, not someone I wanted to be with. I tried to count my blessings. Claire had befriended me when I badly needed it, when my old friends were bitter reminders that there had been life before my brother had died. As an additional benefit, with Claire as my friend I was popular. And when I was popular, people liked me. It was pathetic, really. In some ways, I knew, I was no better than Jo.

The three of us headed down the hallway toward Kyle's locker. A few boys turned to watch as Claire walked by. Sure enough, Kyle was there, fiddling with his lock.

"Need help?" I asked. He looked up. I saw him take in Claire's hair. Something about that bothered me. I guess I wanted him to be different from the other boys, all of whom would have killed to get their hands on that hair, among other sections of Claire's body.

"I can unlock anything," Claire said. She was talking about his locker, but somehow it sounded dirty. How did she do that? Jo giggled.

Kyle looked back at me, and his smile faded. "What, did the headmaster commission you to check up on me throughout the day?"

I cut my eyes at him. Was he really this rude? "That's right," I said. "I forgot you think being nice is lame."

Claire stepped between us. "Give me the combination," she said. She took it from his hand and worked on the lock. Kyle and I were no longer looking at each other, but I

8

could feel the energy between us. I realized I knew nothing about him, like why he'd moved to New Jersey after school had already started. "Voila," Claire said as she pulled the lock open.

"You did it!" Jo cheered.

Claire looked at Kyle. She stood close to him, and I could feel his energy shift from me to her. "Claire," she said. She extended a hand, and he shook it.

"Kyle," he said.

"Welcome to BCD," Claire said. "This is Jo, and you already know Lindsey."

Kyle glanced at me. "Yeah."

"You let me know if you need anything else," she said. "Come on, girls."

I rolled my eyes just slightly, and Kyle saw it. Then we walked away.

"Hot *and* smells good," Claire said. "A winning combo."

"He obviously likes you," Jo said.

"Really?" Claire looked at me. I shrugged. Chances were he did like her. Every other boy at BCD did. "He's not your type at all," she said to me.

"I'm not interested in him."

"It's okay if you are." Since when had he become *hers* to decide whether it was okay if I did? "I just don't think it would work," she added.

"I said I'm not interested. He's a jerk, so you can drop it."

Claire pursed her lips and shrugged. For a brief moment, I wondered if I'd gone too far, said a little too much about what I really felt. Somehow, though, whenever I did, she kept being my friend.

"This looks serious," Missy said. The three of us turned to see her coming from the library. Her round face was bright, still holding some of her tan from the summer. I smiled. Of my three friends, Missy won by a long shot.

"You missed all the fun," Claire told her.

"No," Missy said sarcastically. "I hate missing drama."

"It's not drama," I told her. "Claire met the new guy."

"New hot guy," Jo corrected me.

Missy waved her hand dismissively. "Claire and yet another hot guy," she said. "Call the paparazzi." This was what I loved about Missy. She didn't care what Claire thought. She didn't care what anyone thought.

Claire reached behind Missy and unclipped the barrette holding back her dark, wavy hair. "How many times do I have to tell you your hair is your best quality? Leave it down." Missy grabbed the barrette back from Claire. Then she looped her arm through mine.

"We're going to gym," she said as she pulled me with her. After a few steps, she piled her hair back on top of her head and clipped the barrette in. "Why are we still hanging around with them?" she asked. I smiled as if she were joking, but I knew she wasn't. Because Missy was such a good friend, she had begrudgingly tagged along when Claire adopted me, and Claire had accepted Missy because she knew I wasn't coming without her. But after two years, Missy had gotten tired of the Claire Show. In some ways, I had too. But becoming Claire's friend meant I got to become someone else, someone other than the girl whose brother had died, and I wasn't sure I wanted to let that go.

3

After school, I took the bus to the Weinsteins', whose children I babysat three times a week. They lived in a town house not too far from my family's apartment. After one of my dad's patients killed himself and my dad lost his job at the hospital in a malpractice suit, we had to move from a house in Westwood to the apartment we lived in now. Mom had suggested taking us kids out of private school, but he refused. He said just because he lost a job didn't mean he couldn't provide for his family. He opened a small psychiatry practice soon after, but it was obvious he didn't feel good about things. He stopped making goofy jokes during dinner, and sometimes he didn't make it home for dinner at all. Mark said he was a shit, but I could tell that Dad just felt bad about himself, and that facing us sometimes made him feel worse. That, I would say, was the beginning of the end of my parents' marriage. They fought constantly. And when Mark had his accident, two years ago at age fifteen, just six months after Dad's career was ruined, Mom and Dad turned from each other entirely. In some ways, I understood why Mom left the second she found someone new. Who wouldn't want to leave the disaster our family had become?

I rang the doorbell and heard Laird's pattering feet on the other side of the door. Something crashed from the kitchen.

"Don't you open that door without asking who's there," Mrs. Weinstein called out.

"Who are you?" Laird yelled.

"Hi, Laird," I said loudly. "It's Lindsey."

"It's Lindsey," Laird said.

"Then open the door." Mrs. Weinstein's heels clicked over the tile foyer, and the door opened. She was in silky pants and a yellow sweater, her dark hair pulled tightly back from her face. The baby in her arms pulled at her dangling diamond earring. She greeted me, and I stepped inside. Laird started yelling and ran for the living room, which was an explosion of toys and books. The Weinsteins' was so different from my own home, where everything was organized and quiet. I liked coming here.

Mr. Weinstein came down the stairs, wearing a jacket. He was not a handsome man, but he was always smiling, and I felt drawn to him by that. Sometimes, after they left, I imagined this was my family, Laird and baby Sol my younger brothers. All of us happy and loud, just waiting for our parents to come home.

Once we were alone, I made Laird his dinner of stars and cheese, and I mixed a bottle for Sol. With Laird in his booster seat and Sol in his high chair, I leaned against the stove and ate the rest of the stars and cheese from the pan.

"Why are you eating that?" Laird asked.

"Because I'm hungry too," I told him.

"Don't you have a home?"

"Of course I have a home."

"You don't have food there?"

"Of course I do," I said. "But I'm here now, and now is when I'm hungry." I knew he was asking innocent questions. Still, I dropped the spoon back into the pan and rinsed the pan in the sink. Few things were worse than a kindergartner making you feel as if you had nothing.

Sol started to fuss, so I picked him up. "What's the matter, little guy?" I said.

"He wants you to sing to us."

"He does?"

"Yes." Laird took a sip of milk, watching me.

"How do you know?"

"I know because he's my brother."

I nodded. It was a reasonable answer. I started singing "Twinkle, Twinkle, Little Star." He was right. Sol settled and watched me, mesmerized.

"Not that song," Laird said, interrupting. "Sing one of Daddy's songs."

"I don't know your daddy's songs," I told him. Sol started to fuss again.

"Oh." Laird frowned and looked back at his food. "Then just sing what you were singing."

So I did. Feeling like an outsider once again.

4

The second I walked through the door, I wished I hadn't. Dad's voice boomed from the hallway.

"This is the second time on a school night!"

I set down my backpack as loudly as I could, hoping I'd make enough noise to distract them.

"I don't care," Tara yelled back. Her bedroom door slammed. So much for my attempt at noise.

"You open that door, Tara," Dad said.

Her music came on then, and I went to the hallway and saw him outside Tara's room. A vein popped from his neck. His fists clenched. He banged on the door, and I moved toward him.

"Dad," I said. "I'll talk to her."

He turned to look at me. He was angry, but there was a crease in his forehead too, as if he was afraid. My stomach felt thick and dense. I hated it when he got like this. If he couldn't handle us, who would hold together what was left of this family? I put a hand on his arm.

"It's okay," I said.

He nodded and rubbed his face. "Will you get me some aspirin, hon?"

"Of course." He walked to the kitchen. Tara's music was still blasting, but I knocked at her door. "Tara," I said. "It's me."

"Go away."

"Just let me in for a second."

The knob turned and she opened the door halfway. Her brown hair hung past her shoulders. With her shirt tied above her belly button and her denim mini creeping up her thighs, she looked a lot older than thirteen. "You have exactly thirty seconds," she said.

"Dad works all day and lots of nights too. Why do you have to give him a hard time?"

She slit her eyes at me. "Time's up," she said, and started to close the door, but I stopped it with my foot.

"Just tell me what you did."

"I did nothing, Lindsey."

"You obviously did something. Dad's really upset."

"Fuck Dad," she said.

"I'm serious." I raised my voice a little, getting frustrated now, hoping too that this wasn't about the twenty bucks. "I told Dad I'd take care of this."

"I don't need another mother," Tara said. "And you need to get a life."

"I just want you to stop making things so difficult."

Tara pressed her lips together. She looked like she was about to cry. "You're the one making things difficult."

"No, I'm not," I said, incredulous.

"Remove your foot," she said. I did, and she slammed the door.

Fuming, I went to the bathroom and got Dad the aspirin. In the kitchen, I poured a glass of water and handed it to him.

"I tried talking to her," I said. "I didn't get very far."

He waved a hand dismissively. "It's not your job."

"You have enough to deal with."

He rubbed his face again. He reached toward me, and briefly I thought he might pull me into a hug, but he just patted me on the arm. He'd never been much of a hugger. "I'm fine," he said.

I stood waiting. He didn't say anything about the missing twenty. He didn't say anything at all. Times like that, when it was just the two of us, I wished he would talk to me. I mean really talk to me. About Mark and the fact that he died. Or about Mom leaving and how that felt. But he never did. After a few moments, he got up and went to his bedroom. I heard the door click shut.

Mark's room was open, as usual. The night he died, he was at a Halloween party, and his friend Tim Fanno, a year older than Mark, drove him home. Tim's parents and my parents had been good friends, and Mark and Tim had been friends since grade school. But Tim had been drinking that night, and he took one of the curves on 9W too fast. The car slid out beneath them, and they crashed headlong into a truck coming the other way. Tim got pretty messed up, but Mark was the only one who died. The Fannos sent us fruit baskets every Christmas. They also sent cards every month or so, sending good wishes. But after the accident, my parents didn't speak to them anymore. I guess I understood why. How could they talk to the Fannos when Tim was alive and Mark wasn't?

What I didn't know about my brother's death was whether Mark had been drunk too. Nobody mentioned it. Mark's reputation as the perfect son had to be preserved. But the question of whether he had been drinking or not haunted me. I knew this truth felt vital, though I didn't know why. Either way, he was still dead.

Dad's wallet was on the console again. I picked it up and flipped it open. There was a fresh stack of bills, and I slipped out a twenty. I took it to my room and put it on my nightstand. If Dad hadn't noticed it the first time, I doubted he'd notice it now. I guessed that was just how things worked: people took what they wanted, and nothing changed at all.

5

Thursday afternoon, I went to Ms. Keller's office for an ambassador meeting. There were four of us, one for each grade. Pasha was from ninth grade, Jerome was from eleventh, and Sidney was from twelfth. We all sat quietly as we waited for Ms. Keller, who was always late. The receptionist let us wait in her office, though. As ambassadors, we were trusted more than the other kids.

Sidney smiled at Pasha. "Cute bag," she said, referring to the red Versace in Pasha's lap.

Pasha smiled back. "Thanks. My mom got us matching ones when she was in London."

"Oh," Sidney said. She stuck her legs out in front of her, showing high-heeled snakeskin boots so pointy they made me wonder how she walked. "I got these in London last summer. We go to Europe every year."

"Oh my God," Pasha said, her dark skin glowing under the senior girl's attention. "We do too."

I glanced at Jerome, hoping to share rolled eyes. But he was going over his notes from last week's meeting. I twisted around to see the tall grandfather clock Ms. Keller had in her office. 1:39. Almost ten minutes late. Right then, she opened the door.

"I'm so sorry," Ms. Keller said as she rushed to her desk. Her face was flushed, and she wore a crease in her brow. She was often rushing around, stressed. I wondered why she would choose a job that left her so harried. But I also knew we had to make choices in life we didn't always want. I had said this once to Ms. Keller while we were discussing my future, and she told me my family's situation had matured me. Most kids my age didn't have thoughts like that.

She dropped a pile of papers on the desk and arranged herself in the leather chair. She sighed and pushed her smooth, styled hair from her face. "Those budget meetings can be bears," she said.

Jerome nodded, like he knew what she was talking about. What a kiss-ass. If Missy could see what I had to deal with, she'd make me give up my ambassadorship. But being an ambassador was important to me. It would look good on my college application, and Dad certainly approved of that. It also meant something to Ms. Keller, who I wanted to please.

"Our Ivy school reps are coming in two weeks, Sidney," Ms. Keller began. "Will you help me greet them and set them up in the cafeteria?"

"Of course," Sidney said, writing it down. "Is this Harvard, Yale, and Princeton?"

"And Brown," Ms. Keller said.

"I *so* want to go to Brown," Pasha said.

"You're *so* the Brown type," Sidney answered. Whatever that was supposed to mean. I liked the idea of Brown too, but my plan was Johns Hopkins for premed. It was where my dad went, and where he had wanted Mark to go.

"And, Lindsey," Ms. Keller said. "Mr. Zukowsky is setting up auditions for the school play."

"The play!" I said, excited. Every year, BCD performed two plays, one in the fall and one in the spring. The previous year, as a freshman, I hadn't been allowed to audition. Only tenth through twelfth graders were eligible, the idea being that the experience would add sparkle to their college applications. It felt so unfair at the time, especially since Mark had died the year before and I badly needed a distraction. But now here I was, a sophomore, able to audition.

"A musical, actually. Mr. Zukowsky is doing a production of Rodgers and Hammerstein's *Oklahoma!*"

"Oh." I kept my expression steady, but inside I was bursting. I liked acting, but even more, I loved singing. It was my favorite pastime. When I sang, it felt as though my body emptied itself of any stress and let light in. My whole being lifted, and I forgot about everything else.

Ms. Keller continued, "Mr. Zukowsky needs someone to monitor the hallways during rehearsals, and of course I thought of you."

My heart sank. "Monitor the hallways?" I said. A second ago, I'd imagined myself onstage, belting out "Oh, What a Beautiful Mornin'." Now I was standing all alone, listening to everyone else sing behind the closed auditorium doors.

"Is that a problem?" Ms. Keller asked.

"No, no." I shook my head. "It's just—"

"It's just what, Lindsey?" Ms. Keller began to get her

frantic look, the crease returning to her forehead. "If you can't do it, you need to let me know, and I'll find someone else."

"No," I said. "There's no problem. Of course I'll do it."

Beside me, I could hear Jerome scribbling away. What the hell was he writing? Notes about how I almost lost my ambassadorship? I thought about grabbing the pencil out of his hand and breaking it in two. It would be so unlike me, so impulsive and deviant. But of course I didn't. I sat quietly with the others until the meeting ended. And I left in an orderly fashion, everything in its usual balance.

After school, Missy and I lingered at the drugstore before our buses came. She took the 4, which followed 9W to Englewood Cliffs and Alpine. Almost nobody from school took my bus, the 72, which headed south, toward the Manhattan-commuter towns close to the bridge.

We went to the makeup aisle. I ran my fingers over the smooth compacts and foundation bottles while Missy tried on lipsticks. I didn't usually wear lots of makeup, even though most girls my age did. Mark had had a girlfriend, Caitlin, who never wore makeup, and she'd told me I didn't need to either. She certainly didn't. She had long brown hair and big eyes and inch-long eyelashes. Mark called her "my supermodel girlfriend," which always made her blush. He was like that, complimenting people.

Even me. He said I had a great voice, that I had the talent to become a real singer. Thinking about this now, I felt a deep, terrible ache in my chest.

"What do you think?" Missy asked, pulling me from my thoughts. She had on a dark red lipstick. With her Italian features and coloring, she looked a little like an exotic dancer.

I winced. "Really?" I said.

She laughed. "That bad, huh? What about you? You should wear lipstick sometimes."

I shook my head. "I look like a transvestite when I put on makeup."

"Then you're doing it wrong. Come here."

She pulled out a pale rust-colored lipstick. "Open your mouth a little." I held still while she applied it. She stepped back to see her work. "Lindsey," she said. "You're a total babe."

I looked in the small, smudged, rectangular mirror that was part of the Revlon display. My breath caught. I really did look amazing. "Let me see that." I took the lipstick.

"You should get it," Missy said. Outside, a bus sighed as its door opened. "Shit." She grabbed her bag. "Is that yours or mine?"

I slipped the lipstick into my jacket pocket. It happened in a second, but the moment felt like slow motion. I could feel the rough corduroy of my jacket against my knuckles, then the silky inside of the pocket. I glanced up at the surveillance mirror in the corner of the ceiling. I removed my hand from the pocket, the lipstick a little weight inside. And then everything sped up again. I followed Missy out the sliding doors, my heart a crazy drumbeat in my chest. But no one stopped me. No one even looked at me. My stomach was heavy, but I also felt light and energized, as if I'd just had a shot of espresso.

If Mark could be taken from me, I reasoned, why couldn't I take something too?

6

Claire examined the packaged sushi they'd given us at lunch. Only our outrageously rich school would offer sushi. I was sure every other educational institution in New Jersey was serving corn dogs or pizza, the way any respectable school with no budget would.

"How do we know this is safe?" she asked.

"We don't," said Missy. "Besides, the school shouldn't promote killing sea life. It's unethical."

"You've got to be kidding me." Claire opened her iced tea and took a swig. "Now you don't eat fish?"

"That's a little over the top," Jo said.

I looked down at my own lunch, preparing for this day's episode of the Claire-Missy Debate. Missy was working on a biodiversity project for the winter science fair, so she had some investment in the issue. But, let's face it, the sushi did look pretty gross.

"I haven't eaten fish since I was twelve." Missy tucked a strand of her wavy hair behind an ear. "And neither should you."

Claire smirked and, with her eyes on Missy, popped a piece of sushi in her mouth. "Delicious," she said.

Missy shrugged. "It's your conscience."

"And your stomach," I added, pushing the sushi away. I wasn't opposed to eating fish, but I doubted this sushi was a good idea for anyone.

Claire leaned toward me, her blond hair falling against the table. "Did you hear about Kyle?" she asked.

I raised my eyebrows, trying to look uninterested. Unfortunately, I was a little more interested than I would've liked.

"Oh, yeah," Jo said. "About why he moved here."

I couldn't help myself now. "You know what happened?"

Right then, Sam slid in beside me. "I figured you girls were having a Sam jones," he said as he reached for my sushi. Sam was a royal pain and probably the biggest perv in our grade, but he was also our friend. Because he and Claire went all the way back to preschool together, he had always felt comfortable hanging around her. Having Sam to entertain us was probably the best thing that came out of joining Claire's group.

Claire rolled her eyes.

"Not likely," Missy said.

"Go ahead," Sam said, seaweed stuck to his teeth. "Don't let me interrupt. You were obviously discussing something important."

"We're talking about the new guy," I told him.

"Ah." Sam's small, dark eyes widened. "He's a stud, apparently."

"What did you hear?" Claire asked.

"You first."

Claire smiled her this-is-good smile. "I heard he brought pot to school and got kicked out."

My mouth dropped open.

"Oh, please." Missy laughed.

Sam shook his head. "That's not it at all. He got some girl pregnant. He was a major player."

My mouth dropped further.

"Yes!" Claire clasped her hands together, thrilled with this possibility. "I bet Kyle was at the top of his class, and with scandal looming, his parents scrambled to get themselves out of town. Anything to preserve Kyle's reputation for college." She beamed, pleased with herself.

"Come on," Missy said. "Isn't this a plot line from a CW show?"

"Oh my God," I said. I was shocked, but also disappointed. I didn't know what I'd expected. I was surprised to find I'd expected anything. I guess I didn't want Kyle to be the kind of guy who would do any of those things.

Tara walked into the lunchroom with a group of her friends. They all wore low-slung jeans that showed off the skin above their hips, and they carried tiny purses. They were giggling and whispering about something, their bodies close together. Sometimes Tara reminded me so much of Claire I felt sick to my stomach.

Sam shook his head, bringing my attention back to the table. He looked at Missy. "Let's face it. The guy's a Casanova."

Missy leaned in, conspiratorial-like. "Then why do you and Claire have different stories?"

26

"Maybe they're both true," Jo said.

"Who told you he got anyone pregnant?" Claire asked Sam.

"Olivia Hansen," he said.

Missy laughed, but Claire's expression went flat.

I was connecting the dots. "Who did you hear your version from?" I asked.

Claire twisted her lips. "Olivia Hansen."

Missy laughed harder.

"What?" asked Jo, as though telling two different stories didn't pretty much guarantee they were both lies. As though Olivia wasn't already the biggest liar on the planet.

"Well, if the version I heard is true," Sam said, "I need to find out his secret."

We all looked at him.

"Come on," he said. "The guy got laid."

"Do you ever think about anything else?" Missy asked him.

We all stopped talking as Kyle passed by our table. He waved hello, and Claire flashed him her pearly teeth.

"Kyle," Sam said, grinning. "My man."

Kyle's and my eyes met, and I felt something flutter in my stomach. Claire saw us looking, and her smile faded just slightly.

"Don't let me stop the conversation," Kyle said.

We all looked at one another.

"Uh-oh," Kyle said. "You were talking about me." He put his hand to his mouth, feigning embarrassment and surprise. "Let's see, which rumor would this be about? The

one where I'm a drug dealer, or the one where I knocked up some girl?"

Sam leaned over to touch fists. "Dude," he said.

Kyle hit Sam's fist, but he also shook his head at him, grinning.

"Is everyone at this school so gullible?" Kyle asked.

Sam looked confused, and we all watched as Kyle walked away.

"A classic bad boy," Claire said, keeping her eyes on him as he left through the cafeteria doors. "Who isn't intrigued by that?"

"We don't know that he did anything bad," I said. "Didn't he just deny it all?"

"Oh, that's right, you're BCD's Goody Two-shoes," she said. "You're never intrigued."

"Claire, if you want him, go for it. I'm not getting in your way."

Jo snorted. "Like you could."

I glared at her, but my throat tightened. Of course, Jo was right. I didn't even like him like *that*. I wasn't convinced I liked him in any way. But it would've been nice to believe I could have something I wanted, just that once.

"She's too busy wanting me," Sam told us. "Isn't that the truth, baby?"

I smacked him on the arm. "In your dreams."

"Oh, I've been there." He grinned at me, the seaweed still stuck in his teeth.

"Gross." I smacked him again.

"For the record," Claire said, "I don't want Kyle." It

was an obvious lie. She just didn't want to appear as if she wanted anything. That way, when boys went after her, they'd feel privileged if she chose to be with them.

"Yeah," Sam said. "Because you're also too busy wanting me."

"Look," Missy said. "No one wants Kyle. Let's move on." Sam started to say something. "Nor do they want you," Missy added.

Claire and I locked eyes. "Fine," she said.

As we were leaving the lunchroom, a yellow sign on the bulletin board caught my attention. Auditions for *Oklahoma!*, the following week, in the auditorium. I looked away, trying to avoid the disappointment that was creeping its way back into my chest.

"What's this?" Claire said. She must have seen me looking at the announcement.

"You'd be so good in that play," Jo said to her.

Missy rolled her eyes. "Lindsey's the singer," she said. "You should try out."

Claire and Jo glared at me. Claire used to host singing contests at her slumber parties until she heard my voice. She changed the contests to dancing, knowing I had no coordination.

Two boys from our class walked by slowly, their eyes on Claire.

"Hi, Claire," one of them said. She rolled her eyes and turned back to me, waiting to hear what I had to say.

"As ambassador, I'll be monitoring the halls during rehearsals." I held my head high as I said it, but I realized how lame I sounded.

Claire suppressed a smile. "Too bad," she said. "I'm sure you would have been really good."

"Oh, she's good all right," Sam said, oblivious to the tension. He slipped an arm around my waist and I squirmed away.

"Sam," Missy said. "Do you have anything to contribute to the conversation that is unrelated to sex?"

He shrugged. "Not really."

"At least he's honest," I said.

Missy leaned close to me as we headed for the cafeteria doors. She didn't want Claire or Jo to hear. "Forget the ambassadorship," she said. "This is your thing."

I frowned. "You know I can't."

"Lindsey," she said, but she stopped there. I knew what she wanted to say: I should do things for me for once. I should stop letting other people's needs control my life. She was probably right, but I didn't have Missy's headstrong attitude. Her willingness to take on the world.

"I'm not like you," I said.

"I know." She pushed the door open and waited until Claire, Jo, and Sam had all walked through before smiling wide. "The world can only handle one Missy Grady."

Sam looked back at us before turning down the hallway. "And we thank the Lord for that," he said.

7

In the shower, I sang every song I could remember from *Oklahoma!* While most kids my age listened to Tupac or Modest Mouse, I had listened obsessively to my dad's old show-tune albums since I was little. My favorite was *West Side Story*, about two people who fall in love even though they're completely different. It's my favorite love story of all time.

As I finished the last verse of "People Will Say We're in Love," I turned off the water. Singing in the shower is a cliché, but I liked it. The steam really did open your windpipe, and I also loved the aloneness of it. No one there to distract me. Just me and my voice, rising into the air.

I heard the phone ringing, and then the sound of Tara answering it. Usually, if it was for her, I would immediately hear her talking nonstop. Otherwise, she called out for Dad or me. This time, neither happened, so I knew it was Mom. I quickly dried off, threw on some sweatpants and a T-shirt, and went out to pick up the extension in the kitchen.

". . . to make arrangements," Mom was saying.

"Hi, Mom." I glanced over at Dad, who was researching something on the Internet, but he didn't seem to care. Or maybe he just hadn't heard.

"Lindsey." Mom sounded relieved. I knew I was easier for her to talk to than Tara. Not that I was her favorite. I just didn't clam up or start acting like a bitch, both part of Tara's M.O. with Mom. "Tara and I were just talking about you girls' visit."

"*You* were talking about our visit," Tara corrected her.

"Right, that's what I said." Then I heard a small voice at Mom's end. She said, "I'll be there in a second." We were all quiet a moment. It was Cooper, her stepson, but we didn't dare acknowledge that. It was one of our many off-limits topics of conversation. "Anyway," she went on. "I sent you your tickets."

"Great," I said. But already my stomach felt jumpy. Tara and I had gone to Mom's for Christmas last year after she had moved with Dave to California, and she expected we'd come every year from now on, part of Mom and Dad's custody arrangement. It wasn't that I didn't want to see her. I did. The truth was, I missed her terribly. But seeing her made the missing worse, like the sting when you rub at a paper cut. Sometimes it was easier to pretend our family consisted of just Tara, me, and our dad.

"How are you girls?" Mom asked. Her voice was over-eager. She hadn't figured out yet how to make this normal—calling her daughters from three thousand miles away.

"Like you care," Tara said.

Then again, none of us knew how to make this normal.

"Tara," I warned.

"This is hard for me too," Mom said.

I winced. "Of course it is."

"I'm the one who lost a child." Her voice broke and she started to cry. I took a deep breath.

"Oh, boy," Tara said. "Here we go." There was a click, and it became clear she had hung up.

"I'm sorry, Mom," I said. "Don't cry."

She sniffed. "I know your sister is angry with me," she said through sobs.

"She's just not used to the situation."

She sniffed again and caught her breath. "I know that."

We were silent. My throat ached. I wished, more than anything right then, that I could lay my head against her chest like when I was little.

"Are things okay there?" she asked. I considered telling her I'd stolen twice from Dad and once from a store. I considered telling her I was afraid I wouldn't stop. But that might put her off completely, and then she'd be out of our lives for good. I was the daughter she could count on to be sane. The one who would make sure we got on that plane to see her again.

"Everything's fine," I said.

"You and your sister are doing well in school?"

"Yes."

"Getting homework done on time?"

"Of course." I knew what she was really asking. She wanted to know whether Dad was doing his job as a parent. As if *she* was, living so far away. But that topic was also off-limits. I looked at Dad. He was still consumed by the computer. The truth was, he couldn't get Tara to do anything he wanted, but I didn't say anything about that either.

After we hung up, I peered over Dad's shoulder. He was reviewing abstracts on adolescent drinking. "What's this?" I asked.

He startled when I spoke. He really had been lost in his own world. "I have a parent concerned about her teenager. I'm looking for alcohol interactions with SSRIs." He was talking about antidepressants. I nodded, but I was thinking about Mark. Did Dad think of him when he worked with these patients? Did he know whether Mark had been drinking? I wished I could just ask him, but Dad had his off-limits topics too. What's more, I was scared. Scared Dad had no idea what was going on with Mark before he died. Scared no one had really known him at all.

Dad moved on to the next abstract. He used to engage Mark in this sort of thing. He would call him over and show him the article headings. He would talk to him about cases. It was his way of trying to get Mark interested in medicine. Once, Mark wrote an essay for his English class titled "21 Reasons I Don't Want to Be a Psychiatrist." He had only shown it to me. The paper depicted Dad as selfish and kind of crazy, and I remembered feeling defensive for him. But the essay was also quite good, and Mark earned an A. I wondered if Dad had ever known how Mark really felt. Especially since he expected me to be the psychiatrist now. We had never outright talked about it. It was just assumed that with Mark gone, I would pursue premed. I hadn't wanted to argue. So I silently agreed. And lately, Dad beamed the way he used to about Mark when he told his colleagues about my goals. I knew how important this was to him, to have one of his children succeed where he was afraid he'd failed.

Something entered my mind then, and I wondered if I should say it. So I just did.

"Remember when Mom took over the production of my second-grade play?"

I couldn't see Dad's expression since he was facing the computer. He said, "I do."

"It was *Stone Soup.*"

He nodded.

"And she came out onstage to bow with us at the end."

The image came to me clear as day: Mom in a long black skirt and cowboy boots, facing the cheering audience. She had looked back at us, crossing her arms over her chest as though she were hugging us. It was a shock to remember her this way. She had been so different since Mark's death, closed off and careful, as if something terrible might happen again. I still couldn't see Dad's expression, so I prodded a little more.

"You brought her flowers that night."

This time, he didn't respond. I wondered if he remembered them, the yellow daffodils, and Mom's smile when he gave them to her. Then he said, "Will you get me some aspirin, hon?"

I bit my lip. "Of course." Tears pricked my eyes, and I quickly went to the hallway, not wanting him to see.

8

Claire and I looked through the racks of sweaters. She pulled out a blue mohair shrug and held it to her chest.

"What do you think?"

Like anything ever had a chance to look bad on her. I nodded. "Cute."

"Are you sure?"

"I just said so."

"No, I mean about paying."

"I told you." I looked back through the sweaters. "My dad gave me his credit card and said to bring a friend."

I could feel her watching me. I knew she was thinking that since my dad's malpractice suit, my family hadn't had enough money to take a friend on a shopping spree. I was also the only one of the four of us friends missing a parent at home. Even Jo, whose parents were divorced, had a step-father who got her whatever she wanted. And I was definitely the only one in an apartment. I didn't look up. I didn't want her to see that my father hadn't given me jack. I had stolen the credit card from his wallet the night before.

"Okay." She took the shrug and moved on to skirts. Her long hair hung over her face as she examined sizes. After our lunchroom conversation about Kyle, I wanted to get back in Claire's good graces, but now I was wondering about the intelligence of my plan. She was gathering quite the load in her arms.

I took the sweaters and jeans I'd already chosen and went to the dressing rooms. I closed a heavy door, laid the clothes on the bench, and bent down to take off my boots. When I stood again, I saw myself in the mirror: mousy hair, dark eyes. The girl who stole from her father. I looked away quickly, took off my jacket, shirt, and pants, and pulled a black turtleneck sweater over my head. I put on a pair of distressed jeans. When I looked up, the same girl was still there, staring back at me. I took it all off and yanked on my clothes. I stepped into my boots, leaving the store clothes in a heap on the floor. I just wanted to get out of there. This had definitely been a stupid idea.

"Are you almost ready?" I asked Claire when I stepped out of the dressing area. She seemed to be on her way in.

"I was going to try these on." She held up her pile of clothes, looking perplexed. "Do you need to leave?"

"No, go ahead." What was I going to do? Tell her I had changed my mind?

I kicked myself as I found a seat near the front of the store, wishing I hadn't taken Dad's card. The salesgirl, who had short dyed-black hair and didn't look much older than me, glanced my way, but she didn't look suspicious. Not that I was doing anything. I was just sitting.

When Tara and I had been younger, Mom would take us to the mall for new clothes. Mark never wanted to go, but Tara and I loved it—the hustle and bustle, the perfume smell of the department stores, the tinkling music. And, of

37

course, nothing beat the thrill of finding something new, something that was all ours. Mom said new clothes could transform you, and she always bought at least one thing for herself. Clothes still held that power for me. They could turn me into someone new.

I went back to the dressing room and found the black turtleneck. I just wanted that one thing. What was so wrong about that?

When Claire came out, she was carrying the shrug and two skirts.

At least she had gotten the pile down to three.

"You're sure this is okay," she said again as we stacked the clothes on the checkout counter.

"Yes, I'm sure." But my heart was beating a mile a minute. What would Dad say when he got the bill? The salesgirl rang up the clothes and folded them. I watched the register. $301.00. I felt dizzy as I handed her the credit card. My palms were a sweaty mess. She swiped the card and placed it facedown on the counter. My father's signature sat in plain view. As she put our clothes into a bag, I went to flip the card, but the machine started spitting out the sales slip and she turned back. *Damn.* She ripped off the receipt and placed it in front of me. I felt the salesgirl's eyes on me as I picked up the pen. I leaned over the slip, hoping to cover my handwriting. I hesitated, unsure whether I should write my name or my father's. I decided on my own and scribbled it quickly. My heart pounded as I grabbed the card, smiled, and thanked her.

"Hold on," the salesgirl said as Claire and I were almost out the door.

I could barely hear her over the racket my heart was making. I turned around.

"The receipt says Dr. Nathan Reed."

I raised my eyebrows, my mouth tight. I considered running, but Claire was beside me. I opened my mouth, but nothing came out.

"That's her father," Claire said.

Thank God for Claire.

I nodded.

"He gave her his credit card to use." Claire crossed her arms, holding our bag of clothes.

The salesgirl looked bewildered. Clearly, she was uncertain, which worked to my advantage. "Do you have a note or something?"

"No." I focused on my breathing. In and out, in and out.

"Come on," Claire said. "It's her father. She doesn't need a note." Claire dropped the bag and grabbed for my purse. I held on to it.

"What are you doing?"

"I'm finding something that shows you're a Reed too."

The salesgirl watched us. Her arms hung at her sides. Part of me wanted to give up, just tell the truth. It would have been so much easier. But Claire was here, and I'd involved her. She would not appreciate being put in an unpleasant position. So I joined her in the search for something with my name on it. I found my gym membership, which I never used, and I brought it to the salesgirl. She looked at it and nodded, but she still looked uncertain.

"I need to call my manager," she said.

Claire sighed. I felt like my heart was going to bust. We waited, watching as she dialed the number and got someone on the phone. She nodded, saying "Uh-huh" again and again. Finally she hung up.

"She said I have to call your father."

That dizziness came back.

"You can't," I said quickly. "He's out of town."

I felt Claire look at me.

"Then I have to cancel the transaction."

"This is ridiculous." Claire grabbed my arm and pushed me forward. "Can you not see she is an upstanding citizen? For God's sake, you should see her grades."

I looked down and saw that my hands were clenched into fists. An innocent person would not have clenched fists. I loosened them.

"But my manager—"

"Forget your manager." Claire was riled up now. She was on a roll. "You have your own mind, don't you? Don't let her control everything you do."

The salesgirl bit her lip. Clearly, Claire was trapping her. This was Claire's specialty, getting what she wanted.

"You know you're better than that," Claire said. She smiled, a sweet smile. A you-are-great smile. I knew what it was like to be on the receiving end of that smile. You would do whatever it took to keep it coming, to believe you really were that great. Even when you knew it wasn't the right thing to do.

And that was exactly what happened. The salesgirl looked past us, that nervous expression stuck on her face. "Okay." She clasped her hands. "Just go."

We turned and headed into the busy mall. I felt nauseous and my palms were sweating like crazy, but Claire was energized.

"You're welcome," she said. She grinned at me, still holding the bag.

I grinned back, but a feeling kept nagging at me. A feeling that things were about to spiral out of control. My mind raced. I had at least two weeks to figure out what to do before the bill came. I could blame it on Tara. Or, better, I could intercept the bill before Dad saw it. Panic fluttered at my throat. Maybe this would be it. Dad would find me out. And with that thought, riding just below the panic was the watery feeling of relief.

9

Laird threw the truck to the carpeted floor, where it landed with a thump. "I told you no," he said. He wouldn't look at me, so I crouched down close to him.

"Listen to me, Laird," I said. "You have to brush your teeth before bed. We all do."

"Not me."

"Yes, you too."

He frowned, his eyes on the floor. "I don't want to."

"I know you don't," I said. I reached for his arms, but he shrugged away. "There are some things we have to do, even when we don't want to."

"Why?"

"I don't know why."

He shook his head. "I'm not going to."

"Yes, you are," I said. This time, I picked him up, and he started screaming, writhing in my arms. I held him tight, even though his little legs were kicking at my knees and he was pounding my back with his fists. I was afraid the baby would wake, so I took him into the bathroom and closed the door.

"No!" he screamed. He was heavy, so I sat on the edge of the tub. After about a minute, his body relaxed in my arms, and he started crying. I held him closer as he sobbed into my shoulder.

"It's all right," I whispered. "You're all right."

After a bit, he leaned back and looked at me. Tears stained his cheeks, but he seemed fine. I put him down on the tile floor.

"I'll brush my teeth now," he said.

I squeezed some paste onto his *Finding Nemo* toothbrush. I helped him onto the step stool, and he brushed his teeth over the white sink. He spit and I handed him the matching cup, already full of water. He took a sip, swished, and spit again.

"I wasn't really mad about brushing my teeth," he said after he'd wiped his mouth on a washcloth. He handed me the cup and toothbrush, and I rinsed them.

"No?" I asked. "Then what were you mad about?"

"I want Mommy to brush my teeth with me."

"Ah," I said. I helped him down from the step stool. We didn't say anything more about his tantrum, but I sensed a pressure in my throat. I knew a little bit about how he felt.

10

I stood outside the auditorium, where the auditions were being held. I wasn't going to go in. I just wanted to watch through the open doorway. I could do that, just watch. People were pouring into the room, filling up the seats near the front of the stage. Our auditorium was huge, bigger even than any of the local theaters, and the ceiling was domed, making everyone who spoke onstage sound important and powerful. There were stadium seats and a sound booth in the back, and lights suspended from the ceiling that resembled little stars. Brian Choo, Leslie Betelman, even Olivia Hansen walked in. Claire came too, of course, with Jo by her side. Claire stopped when she saw me.

"Did you change your mind?" She seemed worried, her head held high.

"No. Just watching."

"Too bad." She smiled, relief flooding her face. "Wish me luck."

"You don't need luck," Jo said as they went through the doors.

Then I saw Kyle.

"You can't audition from here," he said.

"I'm not."

"Then what?" He smiled. His teeth were straight and white. "Heckling?"

"Ha ha," I said. "I'm just curious. Is that okay with you?"

He shrugged, but he wasn't being mean. "I'm not your keeper." He stayed there, his hands in his pockets, as a few more people passed. I thought about the way he had mocked the rumors of the pregnant girl and the pot, but he hadn't exactly said they weren't true. I couldn't think of a nonchalant way to ask him.

"I wouldn't have pegged you as the thespian type," I said instead.

"I'm not really." He leaned against the doorjamb. "I'm assistant director. Zukowsky asked me, since I wrote and directed a few plays at my old school."

"You're a writer?"

"I'm more interesting than you think."

I smiled, despite myself. "So the rumors suggest."

He laughed but looked away. Apparently, whatever had happened, it was a sensitive subject. I searched his face. I knew all about sensitive subjects.

"My brother used to write really well," I blurted. I wanted to get us away from the issue of Kyle's transfer, but I immediately wished I hadn't said anything. Why did I have to mention my brother? I didn't want Kyle to label me as the girl with the dead brother, but there was no going back.

"Yeah? What's he write?"

I looked down at my shoes. "Mostly comics. Lots of things."

"He sounds cool."

I nodded, my head still down. A lump in my throat.

"So why aren't you auditioning?" Kyle asked.

Thankful for a new topic of conversation, I looked toward the stage, where Mr. Zukowsky was sitting. Zukowsky was flaming gay and very demanding, which made him the biggest cliché in the world. But everyone adored him. He was funny, and there was something about a teacher who expected a lot from you. It made you want to rise to those expectations.

I didn't want Kyle to know my reasons. Whether the rumors were true or not, he had already made it clear he didn't hold my best-student status in the highest regard. I couldn't imagine he would feel differently about my ambassador duties. "It's not really my thing."

"Then why would you be hanging around the auditions?"

"What is this, Twenty Questions?" I asked. How had this conversation turned so that I was the one on the spot? To my surprise, he appeared concerned.

"Just trying to understand," he said. "That's all."

We both turned to look as the auditorium hushed. Zukowsky was onstage with a clipboard in hand. He described how the auditions would go and went to sit behind the piano at the edge of the stage. I was intensely aware of Kyle beside me. He stood a good foot or two away, but I swore I could feel the heat coming off his body. I willed myself not to look, to keep my eyes straight ahead.

"Ms. Hansen," Zukowsky said. "You're our first victim."

"I should probably get down there," Kyle whispered. "See you around."

I went with him to just inside the door, and then I watched him walk away, noticing the relaxed manner in which he moved, comfortable in his skin. He took a seat near the front, one leg stuck into the aisle. A flutter began its way up my body.

Oh God. I liked him. Like *that*.

Thankfully, Zukowsky started playing the title song, distracting me from my thoughts. Up onstage, Olivia Hansen started giggling. Then she was laughing really hard.

Zukowsky stopped playing. "What is so terribly funny, Ms. Hansen?"

Olivia turned to him, still in a fit of giggles. "I don't know," she said. She wrapped her arms around her middle. "I'll stop."

The whole room watched as she took a breath and erupted into laughter again. "I'm sorry," she blurted.

"Perhaps we should start with someone else." Zukowsky sighed and looked at his clipboard. "Ms. Gregory," he said. "Do us the honor."

Claire stood and shook out her hair. She walked gracefully up the stairs of the stage.

"Go, Claire," Jo called out. Claire looked back, her eyes two darts. She didn't like anyone to disturb her when she was making her big entrance. She nodded at Zukowsky to begin, and he started playing. Claire sang. Her voice was pretty good. I glanced at Kyle, trying to see his expression, but I couldn't see from this far back. He was listening, his head slightly bent. My heart thumped in my chest. I didn't want him to like Claire, like every other boy at BCD.

When Claire finished, everyone applauded. A boy whistled. She smiled demurely and went back to her seat. I turned to go into the hallway, figuring that was all I needed to see. Behind me, the doors closed with a satisfying thud.

11

At home that evening, I couldn't find my protractor, which I needed for my geometry homework, so I went looking for it. Dad wasn't home yet from his office. Tara was in her room on the phone. She had turned on a fan and cold air seeped out from under the door, a clear sign that she was smoking cigarettes. Or something else. I considered knocking, telling her to cut it out, but I didn't feel like taking care of her. Instead I wandered into Mark's room. His bed was against the wall, the same spot where it had always been. Someone had stripped it long ago. Whoever it was had gotten a whiff of his smell. That person might have stood there with the sheets pressed up against their face. Or, more likely, they'd done it quickly, rolling the sheets into a ball and pushing them into a garbage bag, not wanting to endure their scent. I wished I could remember if it was Mom who had taken those sheets off.

On the opposite wall were rows of cardboard boxes, taped shut, full of Mark's stuff. They held his clothes and books and the comics he used to draw, which I'd told Kyle about. Mark didn't like to show them to people, but once I had snuck into his room and found his sketch pad. His characters were long and skinny, and their faces were blurs.

One of the characters was excited as he busily opened a Christmas present. Inside the large box, he discovered a series of smaller boxes nestled one inside the other. The smallest of the boxes contained a tiny rock. At the time, that had seemed awfully sad to me.

Once we had sat in his room for hours drawing joke comics about our parents. Mark drew Mom yelling at Dad to make more money. Dad sat in his office chair. "How does it feel to be so angry?" he asked, a pad and pen in his hands. We had laughed hard at that one. Another one showed Dad handing a little boy a bottle of Prozac. The boy was being led out the door by a stick figure with "X's" for eyes and a straight line for a mouth. "This should get rid of those pesky feelings," Dad said in the comic. Mark had torn up the pictures when we finished, not wanting to get in trouble.

I ran a hand over the box tops. My hand came back dusty.

The desk, his desk, was empty. Before he died, it had always been covered with papers and bike catalogs, none of which he would let me touch. He had a mountain bike Mom and Dad had gotten him for his thirteenth birthday. The bike hung from a hook in the corner of the room. It was another thing that he considered hands-off. Mom couldn't stand that bike because it dropped dried mud onto the carpet, but he loved it. He was often gone, riding trails with Tim. He hadn't wanted to stay in the apartment much.

I didn't like to think about who he would be if he were still alive, whether he would still be biking or drawing comics. I didn't like to think about the fact that he might have done something meaningful with his life.

I pulled out drawers, but they were all empty. What was I looking for anyway? It wasn't as if my protractor would be in here.

I mostly didn't care to think about the fact that he had died when he was my age. That he had feelings and desires and hopes, just as I did, and that now he was gone. And I resented the fact that he didn't have to live trying to be someone for everyone else. He got to do what he wanted. His future hadn't been weighed down by the loss of some-one else's life. It made me mad at Mark when I got thinking like that, so I willed myself to stop.

As I opened the last drawer, something clunked and rolled. I pulled the drawer out further and reached in the back. One of those flesh-colored bouncy balls was in there. The skin was cracked and dirty, but I could still read the word "Pinky."

I held it in my hand. Chances were Mark had been the last person before me to touch it. I guessed this was what I had been looking for: something of Mark's. Something that would tell me more about who he was.

I gripped it with my fingers and squeezed. It gave slightly, then popped back into shape.

A pink ball didn't tell me much of anything.

I closed the drawer again and took the ball back to my room anyway. It wasn't really stealing when the person was no longer alive.

I found an old empty shoe box in my closet and dumped the ball inside. Then I slid the box under my bed.

12

"Have you heard?" Claire asked. She caught up with Missy and me outside school. The huge old oaks on the front lawn had lost most of their leaves, and the limbs were dark and heavy-looking, like thick, tangled hair. The ivy that climbed the brick exterior of the school was mostly bare as well. "Kyle's the new hot commodity." Claire smiled. She wore a white hooded cashmere sweater and Diesel jeans that sat low on her slim hips.

I had on the same jeans jacket I had been wearing since middle school. The same one I told Claire last year was Prada, even though I didn't know if Prada stooped so low as to make things out of denim.

"What are you talking about?" Missy stopped at the steps to take a compact from her bag and check her face.

"Who are *you* primping for?" Claire grinned.

"What does that even mean: hot commodity?" I tried my hardest not to sound desperate at the sound of Kyle's name.

Claire looked at me. "I thought you were supposed to be the smart one."

"Thanks a lot," Missy said.

We climbed the ten steps leading up to the entrance,

and as Missy opened the door, Sam caught it from the other side and held it open. I wasn't totally sure, but I thought I saw Missy blush.

"*Mademoiselles,*" Sam said.

"Do not attempt to speak French," Missy told him.

"Anyway," Claire continued, "apparently, girls are starting to vie for Kyle." She looked meaningfully at me. She wanted it to register that I had competition. It was her way of making me feel insecure, and it worked. How did she know I liked him? Claire never failed to impress me, I'd give her that.

"Good for them." Missy kissed my cheek before turning the corner to walk with Sam to their lockers.

"More like good for him," Claire said, throwing her hair back over her shoulders.

The captain of the lacrosse team strode toward us. He was gorgeous, with big green eyes and blond hair expertly styled to make him look like he had just gotten out of bed. He was a senior this year, and all the girls dreamed of dating him. Of course Captain Lacrosse and Claire had dated on and off since last year, and currently they were off. She had told me once that she kept breaking up with him because she wanted him to have to come after her. Another time, she told me she just wasn't that into him. Claire was the only one of us who'd had a real boyfriend, but even in my inexperience I could see that her behavior was bogus. I knew her well enough to know why she kept up this charade. Whether she liked him or not, she wanted him to keep liking her.

"Hey, Claire. Meet me after school today?" he asked.

He reached for her hand, but she put her arm around my shoulder.

"Can't," she said. "I have plans with Lindsey."

He looked at me for the first time and nodded as if we were business acquaintances. I grimaced back.

"Maybe tomorrow, then?" he asked. "We need to catch up."

"Possibly." She smiled her you're-in-my-way smile, and he ducked his head and walked off. Claire looked at me and rolled her eyes. Poor guy. Watching Claire with boys was like watching a cat with a mouse. She was ruthless.

I got distracted when I saw Kyle at his locker, right next to mine. I took a deep, even breath. Even the way he stood was hot. He had a confidence, a peacefulness, like he fit just right into the world. I hated that I liked him. Not only because Claire obviously did too, and Claire got what she wanted, but because even if he ever liked me back, I knew my father wouldn't let me date. Not when I had class percentiles to top. My stomach felt hollow. I wondered if I could change lockers, just find a way to put some distance between us so I wouldn't have to think about him. I made a mental note to talk to Ms. Keller.

I was quickly distracted again, though. Someone was crying, her head in her hands. Three girls gathered around her, girls I had been friends with before Mark died. They rubbed her back and cooed.

"Looks like Jory forgot her antidepressants today," Claire said.

Jory Gregor. It was no secret she'd been seeing my dad for therapy since she'd been a little kid. She had given a

54

speech about depression at a school meeting last year, and I was impressed that she had been willing to expose herself so publicly. It had gotten me thinking that maybe *I* needed to talk to someone. I would have liked to confide in someone too.

"Maybe something happened to her," I said.

Her crying softened, and she let one of her friends hug her. I felt sorry for Jory and was about to say so, but Claire had moved on. She had spotted Kyle.

"Everyone thinks I'm getting the part of Laurey," she told me. "That's the lead."

"I know who Laurey is."

Claire smiled, her eyes still on Kyle. "Kyle's the assistant director. Did you know that?"

"No," I said. I hated when I did that, lied so Claire could keep feeling superior.

We reached my locker. Claire stopped with me, as I knew she would.

"Hello, Kyle."

He turned to look at us. "Happy Monday," he said. "Hey," he added, addressing just me.

I couldn't speak, but of course Claire could. "Tell that to Jory. I don't think that girl could be happy on a Monday or any other day." She nodded toward the soft crying, and Kyle frowned. I focused on opening my locker.

"You're posting auditions results today, right?" Claire asked.

"By noon," he said.

"People are saying I'm a shoo-in for Laurey, but I don't think that's true. Olivia Hansen has a great voice."

"I guess you'll have to wait and see."

"Come on," she said, and hit him playfully on the arm. "You won't even drop a hint?"

"Not a chance."

I got my locker opened and stared at the mess of papers and books. I didn't want to see Kyle and Claire interacting. It was too obvious they would wind up together. Like with everything else, Claire would get her way. I pushed my stringy hair behind an ear, took a few books, and slammed my locker closed.

When I looked back up, Kyle's eyes were on me.

"You should have tried out," he said.

I bit my lip, not sure how to respond.

"Lindsey couldn't try out," Claire said, blowing my cover. "She has to be a hall monitor."

I pressed my lips together. It sounded so unbelievably idiotic, hearing Claire say it. I wished I could climb into my locker and shut myself inside.

"What do you mean?" Kyle asked.

"I'm an ambassador," I started to explain. "That's why I showed you around on your first day." Claire listened with mock eagerness, her eyebrows raised. Kyle looked confused. "Just forget it," I said. My face was hot with embarrassment, and I walked off to class.

After lunch, people crowded at the bulletin board outside the auditorium. Everyone was already congratulating Claire when I arrived.

"You got it, right?" I said. Jo was beside her, glowing.

Claire nodded and flipped her hair over her shoulder. "My life is about to get very busy," she said. "Rehearsals every afternoon, you know."

I tried to smile. I didn't want to be jealous. I was so deeply sick of being jealous, but I felt I should have been the one with the lead part. Claire's voice was good, but mine was better. Much better. So here I was again, the envy thick in my stomach. "I'm happy for you," I lied.

Claire hugged me. "Thanks, Lindsey." A few girls glanced at us. I knew *they* were jealous of *me*, getting hugged by Claire, the most popular girl in tenth grade. A part of me wanted to end it then. To tell Claire I was done being friends with her, that I'd put up with enough of her manipulations. But the rest of me knew I didn't have the guts. As with everything else in my life. Without Claire and the past two years of subsequent popularity, I was just me. And just me was not who I wanted to be.

Kyle walked up.

"Congratulations, Claire," he said. "Guess you're not disappointed."

Claire kissed his cheek, clearly surprising him. He took a step back and his cheeks flushed.

"Thank you," she said. "It'll be BCD's best play, you'll see."

He nodded. It occurred to me they would be spending every afternoon together now. I hated my life more than ever.

"Too bad about the ambassador thing," Kyle said. "Bet you would have gotten a part."

"What makes you think that?"

Claire watched us, unsure how to enter the conversation.

"I'm thinking there's more to you than meets the eye."

My face felt warm, and I looked down.

"See you guys later," he said, and he was gone.

"Well," Claire said, watching him go. She didn't say
anything else. And I didn't dare look at her.

"Better get to class," I said, and I walked away, allowing
my smile to surface.

13

A few days later, Missy leaned close to the bathroom mirror, checking for mascara goop in the corners of her eyes. When had Missy started wearing mascara? I wondered. I washed my hands. Behind me, some senior flushed and came out of a stall. She washed her hands, reapplied lipstick, and then slung her Louis Vuitton bag over her shoulder. She smirked at me as I moved aside to let her pass.

"Claire's on a mission," Missy said after the girl left, continuing the conversation we had been having since we entered the bathroom. She dug through her bag as she spoke, leaning it against the rim of the sink. "Operation Make-Kyle-Mine."

I glanced at myself in the mirror, trying not to reveal how much I hated hearing this. I thought about telling her what he had said to me: *There's more to you than meets the eye.* But Missy didn't even know I liked him yet.

Bordering each mirror was a wavy gold pattern, as if this were the Four Seasons Hotel and not a high school. Sometimes I wondered what I was still doing here, attending a school so different from my apartment, where the kitchen was no bigger than this bathroom. Before Dad's malpractice suit, it made sense for me to be here. Like most everyone else, I lived in a big house in the right part of town. Things had changed, though. Somewhere between Dad's legal problems, the divorce, and Mark's death, I had become a girl who didn't fit.

I couldn't really be disappointed that Claire would get what I wanted. It was the natural order of things.

"She's obsessed," Missy went on. "God help the boy on the other end of that."

"Doesn't Kyle like her back?" I asked, even though I was afraid of the answer.

"In Claire's mind, there's no such thing as a boy who doesn't."

I knew Missy was right. Why would Claire doubt herself this time? Everyone from Captain Lacrosse to the nerdiest boy in school lusted after her. She had no reason to think Kyle wouldn't want her too. "Maybe there's a chance Kyle's different from every other guy on the planet." I frowned. Even I could hear how unlikely that seemed.

Missy looked at me carefully. "You seem terribly interested in this subject."

"I do not."

"Huh," Missy said. "That's not what I'm hearing."

I ran my fingers through my hair, wishing it would do something other than just hang there, and I tried to sound more like someone who didn't care. I *wanted* badly to not care. "What is she saying about it?"

"They're becoming friends. That's all I know."

I backed away from the mirror. My flat hair and dull skin were doing nothing to make me feel better about Kyle.

I reminded myself to put in for a locker change this afternoon when I saw Ms. Keller at our ambassador meeting.

I watched as Missy applied lip gloss. "Lip gloss?" I asked. I couldn't help myself. Missy wearing makeup was just weird.

Missy shrugged. "I'm just seeing what I look like." She capped the lip gloss and dropped it back into her bag. "Let's go," she said. But I knew Missy. She was being evasive, leaving me a code to unravel. I was used to that, to the blurriness of things. I was used to feeling a million miles away from the truth. But I had never felt that way with Missy.

At the end of the ambassador meeting, Pasha, Sidney, and Jerome stood to leave. Pasha and Sidney were on their way to the cafeteria to set up for the arrival of the Ivy reps. They chattered about the schools as they walked out. I stayed seated, waiting.

"Was there something else you needed, Lindsey?" Ms. Keller asked. She flipped through some papers on her desk, moving on to the next thing.

"Actually, yes," I said.

She licked a finger and held back a page as she read something. I figured I had better just ask.

"I'd like to switch lockers."

Ms. Keller seemed puzzled. "Is there something wrong? Is it broken?"

"Nothing like that."

"Then what's the problem?"

It was clear that my real reason, to get away from Kyle because I liked him and would never be able to have him, was not going to fly. I racked my brain, trying to think of something that would make her comply.

"I think someone's stealing things out of it," I said. I held my gaze steady, hoping she wouldn't see the lie.

She let go of the paper. "This is very serious, Lindsey."

"I'm sure if I just changed lockers, it would stop."

Ms. Keller took a breath. Her brow creased. She slid open a drawer in the file cabinet behind her and riffled through the files until she found what she was looking for. She took out a piece of paper and laid it on her desk. Then she ran a finger down the names on it until she got to mine. I peered at the paper: locker combinations for everyone at school. "I suppose we could find you a new one," she said. She wrote a locker number and combination on a Post-it and handed it to me. "Here," she said. "This one is free."

A knock came at the door, and the receptionist peeked in. An angry adult voice in the background came through the opening. "I'm sorry to bother you," the receptionist said, looking worried, "but we're having a bit of a parent emergency out here."

Ms. Keller stood, that frantic look of hers appearing. "I'll be right back," she said to me as she walked out. She stopped suddenly at the door. "Will you put that list back in its file for me? I left it open." She pointed to the open drawer, where a manila folder sat at an angle to keep her place.

"Of course," I said.

I picked up the list and went to the file. But rather than

putting the paper in, I just stood there in front of the open drawer. I could hear Ms. Keller talking calmly to the parent. My heart beat fast. My fingers tingled. The list I held was a copy. There were at least ten other copies of the same page in the file. I slid the file the right way, closed the drawer, and went to my bag. And I slipped the copy of the list in.

"Tell Ms. Keller I'm all set," I said to the receptionist on my way out. The pulse in my head was so loud, I was afraid she would hear it.

14

Dad and Tara were at it again. His voice boomed through the apartment as he stood at her closed door.

"I said open this door, young lady."

"Fuck you!" Tara yelled over her music, which was loud and thrashing.

I read the same sentence in my history book for the eighth time. Finally, I went to the kitchen and poured myself some juice.

"Are you trying to make me look bad?" Dad said.

Tara's music screamed through the door.

Bang! Bang! Bang! "Open up!"

The phone rang, but when I answered it, Tara was already on with one of her friends.

"Tara," I said. "Get off the phone and come out here."

"Get off the phone and come out here," Tara mimicked. Her friend erupted into giggles. I sighed and hung up.

I went to Dad instead. His hair was sticking out, like he'd forgotten to comb it today. I took him by the arm and led him away from Tara's room and to the kitchen. I got him his aspirin and a glass of water, and I sat down with him.

"You're such a good girl." He smiled weakly and put a hand on one of mine for a moment.

"What did she do?" I asked.

He shook his head and sighed. "She took my credit card. Ran up a three-hundred-dollar bill."

My throat tightened. The bill had come. I was so preoccupied with Kyle I had forgotten to look for it. And now Tara was getting blamed. I looked down at the Formica table, rubbed at a blue pen mark.

"She's out of control," he said. He rubbed his face. "It's not good that I have to go out of town this weekend."

"You're leaving?"

"Just for the weekend. I have a conference. You can handle things for me here, right?"

I got up to get dinner started. But something was nagging me. Why was I always the one making dinner? Why couldn't Dad do it sometimes? I was the one with three AP classes. I yanked open the produce drawer in the fridge and took out broccoli. I grabbed the Parmesan cheese and got a pot to boil water for pasta. I knew I was being a baby, but I was tired of being the good one. I almost told him it was me, not Tara, who took the card. Instead I said, "Of course. I always do."

Dad smiled, not hearing my frustration. I could call Children and Family Services, I thought as I filled the pot with water. But what would I say? My father doesn't acknowledge me? He expects me to take care of things now that our mother's not around?

I set the pot on the burner and turned on the stove. I bit my lip. "What are you going to do about the credit card?" I asked.

He shook his head. "I'm at a loss, Lindsey," he said. "What do you think I should do?"

I looked past him out the window. I would have liked to throw that pot across the room, watch the water explode, hear the pot clatter against the wall. Mom was right. He wasn't doing his job. Why couldn't he just be a father for once?

"Why don't you call the police?"

He looked at me, surprised. The words were barely out of my mouth and already I was afraid he would actually follow my advice. But I had nothing to worry about. He would never risk his reputation. He shook his head. "I don't need to go that far."

A small part of me was disappointed. It would have been good to just end this thing once and for all. If someone else didn't stop me, who would?

"I'll just ground her again."

I shook my head. Tara never cared when she was grounded; she still did whatever she liked. Besides, grounding her wouldn't matter if he was going out of town, I wanted to tell him. But I kept my thoughts to myself. What was the point of saying anything? Nothing changed, no matter what I did.

In my room, I put on my headphones and started to sing. I lay on my bed, closed my eyes, and let loose, allowing all thoughts to evaporate from my mind. But halfway through "Shall We Dance?" a loud pounding started. I yanked off my headphones.

"What!" I yelled.

"Shut *up!*"

Tara.

So much for that.

15

I slipped it into my pocket, the movement so fast, it was like nothing had happened. I kept my eyes steady. My body was relaxed. I didn't even know what it was I'd taken. Just something. A key chain or a pack of gum. It didn't matter what it was. I was doing it for the taking, not the thing. Filling my pocket, even with something small, weighted me down. Fastened me to the earth so I wouldn't up and float away. So I'd know I was really here.

I'd gotten good at this.

Dad was gone for the weekend. Tara was living it up, parent-free. Mom was on the other side of the country, bringing up someone else's kid. In half an hour, I was meeting Missy for a bite at El Taco Loco, a ten-minute bus ride away. So what else did I have to do?

I walked out of that store. On to the next. But as I stepped onto the sidewalk, I saw him coming out of Starbucks across the street. Kyle. What was he doing in this part of town? I thought about ducking back into the store, but he saw me too and waved. I did a quick inventory: I was in jeans and a sweatshirt. My hair was unwashed and in a ponytail. A zit was forming next to my nose. I stupidly, ridiculously liked him. And, of course, my pocket was full of things I hadn't bought. No, nothing about seeing Kyle right now was good. But it was no use. He raced across the street, coffee in hand.

"What a surprise," he said when he reached me. We stood on the sidewalk in front of the store. His curly hair was wet, fresh from a shower.

"That's what I was thinking." I tried to angle my face so he couldn't see the zit. "What are you doing here?"

He laughed. "What do you mean? I live in this area."

"You do?" I said, unable to suppress my smile. "I do too."

He gestured toward the store. "Shopping?"

"Sort of."

We were silent, looking at each other, but he wore a funny expression.

"What's it going to take to crack your code, Lindsey Reed?"

My face grew warm. "I don't know what you're talking about," I choked out.

"You have secrets, and I want to know what they are."

My throat tightened. "No, you don't."

"You lost your brother in a car accident," he said then. "The one who made comics."

I couldn't look at him. I wasn't sure if I could even breathe. I focused on the sound of the cars zooming by to get out my question: "How did you find out?"

"Claire told me. I'm sorry, Lindsey. I feel bad now about saying he sounded cool. . . ."

He didn't finish the sentence. I could feel my tears, and

I blinked fiercely. No way would I cry in front of Kyle. "It's fine," I said.

We went silent again, and he looked out over the street.

"Life isn't always easy," he said. "If anyone knows that, it's me."

I watched him, his handsome face. I wished I had something to say that would bring us closer, but I just stood there. My heart felt heavy. It was what always happened once Mark was mentioned. It was as though I was living a muffled, hazy life, then *bam!*—I was reminded of who I really was, wrapped inside all that gauze.

"I should probably go," I said.

He looked just the tiniest bit disappointed. I winced, berating myself for pushing him away rather than pulling him in. "I'll see you around, though?"

"Sure," he said. He smiled openly, and then I watched him look both ways as he trotted across the street and down the sidewalk. I wondered what he meant when he said *If anyone knows that, it's me.* Maybe we weren't so different, after all.

I found Missy waiting for me at the counter at El Taco Loco. We hugged and ordered veggie burritos, then found a booth near the window.

"How's the biodiversity project coming?" I asked.

"Did you know our nation is stripping South American rain forests?" she asked back.

"I remember hearing something about that." I took a bite of my burrito as she prattled on.

"Sometimes I wonder what the use is in learning anything. It just makes me more and more angry," she said.

"I know what you mean," I said, though I didn't really. I hadn't been truly angry in ages. And when I had, it wasn't about something like the rain forest.

"I don't understand how people can operate without any regard for others."

I nodded. That I could relate to. "They do, though, Miss."

"That's why I like you." She smiled. "You're not like that at all. You try to do the right thing. It's admirable."

I examined my burrito, thinking of the little items in my pocket. "I'm not that admirable."

"You're also self-deprecating," she said. "Which is better than conceited. Unlike Claire."

"Let's change the subject," I told her.

She eyed me and took a bite of her burrito. I knew she hated it when I avoided things. It was the complete opposite of her. "Okay, then. How are your AP classes going?"

"They're okay."

But she must have seen something in my face because she said, "What's going on with you lately?"

"Nothing." I wanted to tell Missy everything. She was my best friend, and I needed someone to talk to. "It's that guy, Kyle."

"Claire's Kyle?"

"He is not Claire's," I said defiantly.

She put down her burrito. "When are you going to admit you like him?"

"I don't like him."

70

"You can't hide from Auntie Missy," she said. "You know that."

"Well, I can't like him," I said.

"Because?"

I bit my lip. "Claire likes him too."

"Claire doesn't like him." She took a sip from her soda. "She just doesn't want you to have him."

I frowned. "Why?"

"Linds," Missy said, leaning toward me. "Are you that naïve? She doesn't want anyone to have anything she doesn't already have. Especially you. She's always been jealous of you. Ever since you got that award."

She was talking about eighth grade, when everyone thought Claire was a shoo-in for the Citizenship Award. The faculty voted on academic achievement, classroom behavior, and the students' likeability among their peers. At the awards assembly, Claire had been outraged by their decision. But she also invited me to her house that day, and we started to become friends.

"But Claire can have anything she wants," I said, getting back to Kyle.

"She didn't get the ambassadorship either."

"With boys she can have what she wants."

Missy sighed. "That's how she likes to make it look. Really, though, she's only playing games with them. She reels them in by batting her eyes and throwing around her blond hair, and then gives them nothing. She's like some kind of ice princess."

I looked out the window and considered this. The wind had picked up, and the few leaves remaining on the small trees along the sidewalk whipped around in a crazed, attention-getting dance. For some reason, I thought of my mother in California. Maybe moving west with another man made it easier to convince herself that she could leave the loss of her son behind. It wasn't that different from Claire, manipulating things to look a certain way. Suddenly I wondered if it was all that different from how I kept a part of myself hidden, just like Kyle said, a part that felt wild and unruly. A part I didn't even know.

When I got home, there was a card from the Fannos in the mailbox. The family of Tim, who had been driving the night Mark died. I guessed it was about time for one to arrive. I knew the return address by heart: 301 Parker Street. One of the big homes north of the school. I gripped the yellow envelope and walked into the elevator, then down the corridor to the apartment door. I turned my key in the lock and pushed the door open. I took off my sweatshirt and shoes. The apartment was silent, nobody home. There was nothing left to do but open the card. I sat on the couch, slid my fingers under the envelope flap, and pulled it out. The front showed a bouquet of pale orange and yellow flowers, held in someone's hand. The inside was handwritten:

Wishing you good things for the fall season.
The best always, Diane, Jeff, and Tim

P.S. Please call if you need anything at all:
555-3082.

I stared at the words, feeling the usual disappointment creep across my chest. Not that a stupid card could somehow change the fact that Mark was dead, or somehow give me the answers to questions I couldn't even express. Not that they ever did, each time they arrived. Still, I carried the card to my room, pulled out the drawer in my desk, and added it to the small pile of their cards I already had.

16

Claire tried to get my attention as we sat in the library, but I ignored her by keeping my head in my AP Chemistry book. I was still upset that she had told Kyle about Mark, as though the fact of his death was hers to tell, like everything else that she took as her own. Finally she leaned over and wrote something in my notebook. I sighed and looked up. It wasn't like the combustive elements were really keeping my interest anyway. She had written: *Kyle's coming over this evening to help me with my lines.*

Good for you, I scribbled back. But inside, I wanted to die.

She smiled, satisfied.

What a bitch.

Later, while she and Kyle were in the auditorium, becoming best buddies, and I was stuck like an idiot out in the hallway, I crouched to open my bag and saw it: the list of locker combinations.

I had almost forgotten about it.

I glanced around. The hallway was empty. Everyone was either in rehearsal or long gone. I slid out the paper and ran my finger over the numbers. That quickening started in my chest and I stood. The low heels of my boots clicked on the tile floor as I approached a locker and looked for the number on the page. I avoided seeing the name, just went to the combination. I turned the dial, once, twice, three times, and the locker opened. I reached in and grabbed something: a velvet headband. And then I shut the door. The slam echoed in the hall and I looked around, my heart battering at my chest.

I slipped the headband into my bag.

No problem.

Tara walked through the door a little after eleven. I sat on the couch, wringing my hands, waiting for her. We hadn't spoken since Dad blamed her for the credit card.

"You're late." I figured this was a good place to start.

"And you're a phony." She set her purse on the floor and shook out her long, dark hair. Her jeans sat low on her hips, showing a thick band of skin beneath her shirt.

"Tara—" I started. But she interrupted.

"You took Dad's credit card and let him ground me. What kind of psycho does that to her sister?"

I bit my lip, trying to think of something to say to redeem myself. Nothing came to mind. She was right. What kind of a sister was I?

"I've got you now." She tilted her head and pointed to me. "You're mine."

I laughed nervously. "Don't be so dramatic. You don't have anything. You have no proof it was me."

She made slits of her eyes. "I could get proof."

I remembered then that I'd signed my name to the sales slip. Why had I been so stupid? But I kept my gaze steady. "There's no proof to get."

She grabbed her purse and walked off toward her bedroom. "We'll see," she called out.

I didn't respond. But inside I began to squirm.

17

Rehearsal time. I went quickly down the hall again, my heart in my throat. Turned the dial three times. Voila. This time, I took a Ralph Lauren scarf. The next afternoon, two CDs.

At home, I stuffed them into the box under my bed, not wanting to see them.

The following day, rehearsal was canceled. Zukowsky's cat was having emergency surgery. Apparently, it couldn't keep down any food. I waited for my regular bus in the rain. A few other kids waited at the same stop, huddled under umbrellas. The sky was a white sheet, and the trees were almost black with wetness. In the parking lot, the seniors ran to their cars—brand-new SUVs and BMWs—while teachers ran to their Hondas and Ford Escorts. Several Mercedes sedans lined up to pick up the younger kids. A little farther down, Claire and Jo waited for their ride. In the distance, Kyle made his way down the sidewalk, toward the bus stop. Toward my bus stop. The wind blew, sending rain into my face, and I swallowed, pulling the hood of my raincoat tighter. I had forgotten Kyle would be leaving early too, and that he would be taking my bus. I looked down the street, trying to seem unconcerned.

"Nice weather we're having," he said when he got there. He had no hood, no umbrella. Just a cotton jacket. His wet hair hung around his face.

"You obviously didn't watch the Weather Channel before school today."

"It didn't rain like this in Vermont. It was sunny or it was snowing." He glanced up at the sky, and I pushed myself to continue talking.

"It must be hard to have to switch schools like that."

He looked at me as kindly as he had the day he told me he knew about Mark. "It's not so bad."

I started to feel anxious. What was wrong with me? Why couldn't I just talk to him like a normal person? Why was I so scared? I watched the rain make little circles in the puddle at the curb, widening and overlapping, moving together and apart.

"Rehearsal was canceled," Kyle said finally.

"I know." I raised my hand. "Hall monitor."

"Right."

We looked down at the puddles forming. Kyle splashed one a little with his foot.

"I'm sure Claire was upset," I blurted.

I watched as he turned to see Claire. She held a black umbrella and was laughing with Jo. Even in the rain, somehow her hair looked soft and silky, her clothes were perfect. She didn't have on some stupid raincoat or a hood covering a head of now-frizzy hair. Seeing his eyes turned toward her, I couldn't stop myself.

"She's pretty, don't you think?"

78

I waited, my stomach tight with jealousy, full of disdain for myself.

He shrugged. "No one could argue with that."

I frowned, the ugly feelings churning. I wished I could stop, but as with stealing, something inside me was loose, fluttering in the wind like the flag in front of the school. "You should ask her out."

He laughed, but it was a bewildered laugh. "Why should I do that?"

"Because she likes you."

He looked at me, an odd expression on his face. "Do *you* think I should ask her out?"

I willed myself to meet his eyes. "I think you should do whatever you want to." The words came out angry, and I could see in the small way his expression changed, from confusion to amusement, that he knew I liked him. I took a breath and looked away, relieved to see the bus finally rumbling toward us. "The bus," I said, just wanting to say anything.

To my relief, the bus was crowded and there weren't two seats together. I found a seat far away from him, and when my stop came, I kept my eyes forward as I sauntered down the aisle and descended the stairs. But as I walked toward my apartment building, something impelled me to look back. And when I did, there he was in the window, watching me go, that same amused expression on his face.

18

On Saturday, Claire called about seeing a matinee. We waited in line for popcorn after buying our tickets. Suddenly I saw curly brown hair at the front of the line.

"It's Kyle," I blurted. If I had thought it through, I would have said nothing.

"Really." Claire rose on tiptoes to get a look. "Kyle!" she yelled.

He turned and came over.

"Here for *Ruby Red*?" Claire asked. That was the movie we were going to see.

"Actually, I'm here for *Dumbo Returns*." He smiled, those dimples popping.

Claire smiled thinly. "You're a laugh a minute."

He looked at me, but I was embarrassed to see him after what had happened at the bus stop. He knew I liked him, and he knew Claire liked him too. What could one say?

"I'm serious," he said. "I'm here with my baby brother for *Dumbo*." He nodded toward a little boy, no older than six, who had the same curly hair as Kyle's. He wore a cowboy hat.

"You have a baby brother?" I asked. I couldn't contain my smile.

Kyle shrugged. "Yeah." He seemed defensive all of a sudden. "I'll see you girls later."

And that was when I saw it. There was something different about his brother. Slanted eyes, doughy skin. His brother had Down syndrome.

"Kyle," I said, but he had already walked off. We watched as he gently took his brother's hand and disappeared down the hall.

"Wow," Claire said. "*There's* some information we didn't have before."

"Let it alone," I told her.

"That's right." She smiled at the popcorn boy behind the counter as we stepped up. "I forgot you're Miss Citizenship. Always doing the right thing. And we don't want to say anything un-PC, do we?"

I was too overwhelmed to respond. Because I had seen Kyle with his brother. I'd had a glimpse into why he said life wasn't always easy. A part of his life was obviously filled with his own aches. Just like me.

Fifteen minutes into our movie, I felt something brush my arm. I turned, and there was Kyle. My stomach dropped, but he just smiled. His brother was in the seat next to him, still wearing the hat and eating popcorn from a bag.

"I don't think he cares which movie we watch," Kyle whispered.

My face turned warm. Claire leaned forward and saw him there, and she frowned. She didn't like him sitting next to me and not her.

"What is this?" Kyle slumped down in the chair. "Some chick flick?"

His legs fell open, and his knee rested against my leg. I held my body perfectly still, afraid he would move his leg but also afraid he wouldn't. The spot where our legs met was on fire.

"It's about a woman who wins the lottery and then loses everything she cares about," I said softly.

"Yawn. Money doesn't make you happy." He snorted.

"Shhh." Claire looked angrily at us both. I knew she didn't really care about the noise. She just didn't like us talking without her.

I leaned closer to him. "Nobody told you to leave *Dumbo*," I whispered. When he looked at me, I smiled. He smiled too, then reached a hand toward his brother.

"Share some popcorn, buddy."

His brother held the bag out to Kyle.

"What's his name?" I asked.

"Zachary." Kyle watched me. He was protective, I could tell. My insides felt like popcorn themselves, bursting and sparking and filling. I smiled at Zachary and leaned forward.

"Hey, Zach," I said. "Cool hat."

Zach smiled, popcorn stuck between his teeth. He reached into the bag and put more in his mouth. I sat back and tried to focus on the movie, but I could feel Kyle beside me, our legs still touching. Then, without any warning, he took my hand. His hand was warm and soft, and he looped his fingers through mine. I turned to look at him, but his eyes were on the screen. I looked down at the outline of his knuckles, the way his veins popped and shifted as he adjusted his hand. I glanced at Claire. She was watching the movie too, but her mouth was set in a line.

Kyle and I sat like that, with our hands entwined, through the whole movie. My hand grew numb, but I didn't dare move it. I tried to focus on the screen and, when that didn't work, on my breathing.

As soon as the credits started rolling, Kyle pulled his hand back and stood. He waved at Claire, and then he hustled out of the row with Zachary. My hand was sweaty from holding his. I rubbed it on my jeans.

"Well," Claire said as we left. "I guess Kyle likes you."

I smiled.

We walked through the lobby, but really I was floating, gliding above everyone else. Sure, my family life stank. But Kyle, the boy I liked, liked me back. Maybe life was getting better. I wasn't going to let Claire ruin this for me. Amazingly, though, she didn't say another word. She just walked, eyes straight ahead, through the exit doors.

19

Back at home, Tara was out, completely disregarding the fact that she was grounded. Dad wasn't home either, so it wasn't like he cared. I hung up my coat and kicked off my shoes. Sometimes I swore I hated my father. But I also didn't want to hate him. In many ways, he was the only parent I had. I went to my room and pulled out homework. Even through my anger, thoughts of Kyle flooded my mind. His dimples, the way his hand felt so warm wrapped around mine.

I put on my headphones and sang for a while. Feeling good.

Then I went to find the phone. I had to tell Missy what had happened. But before I could dial, it rang.

"Is this still the Reed residence?" It was a woman's voice I didn't recognize.

"Yes."

"This must be Lindsey, then. Or is it Tara?"

I gripped the phone. "Who's calling, please?"

There was a beat of silence, and I somehow knew who it was. "This is Diane. Diane Fanno. I'm Tim's mother."

I ran my foot back and forth over the carpet, making an arc. My chest was tight, my heart loud in my ears.

"I'm sorry to call out of the blue," she continued. "I know we haven't spoken in a long time. But Tim was home from college this past weekend. He found something of Mark's in his room. I wanted to get it to you."

"Something of Mark's?" I was having trouble speaking, and she heard it.

"Perhaps I shouldn't have called."

I felt angry. How could she call? How could she mention that her son was in college, while Mark—who would have been a high school senior this year, who might have been going to college next year—was gone? It was a terrible thing to think, but I wished in that moment it had been Tim who'd died.

"Perhaps I'll just send it."

"What is it?" I squeezed my eyes shut, waiting.

"It's a key chain."

"A key chain?" I asked. "You called about a key chain?"

She was silent again.

"We don't want it," I told her.

She cleared her throat.

"Please don't call here again," I said softly, and hung up the phone.

I was fuming. Instead of heading to my room, I went to my dad's bedroom. I walked to his dresser, looking for something, anything, to take. He deserved it, not being here. Leaving me to answer the phone. Expecting me to take over not only Mark's role, but his too. Expecting me to take care of everything, while no one ever seemed to take care of me. I didn't see much, just pennies and receipts. I pulled open a drawer and stuffed my hand inside. Near the back, behind his socks, I felt something small and solid. A ring. His wedding ring, from when he and Mom were married. Tears burned my eyes and I put it in my pocket.

Back in the hallway, I saw Mark's open door. The apartment was quiet, the refrigerator humming. The air was still. I stood, my arms at my sides, and I realized I was waiting. Waiting for something, but for what I didn't know.

At the Weinsteins' Sunday afternoon, I had a hard time keeping my mind in the present. Sol was napping, and Laird and I were playing, but my head was swirling with too much stuff, with Kyle and the phone call. With things no five-year-old cares about.

"You're no fun today," Laird said frankly.

"You're right." I put away the blocks we were using to build a tower, and I went to his parents' CD collection.

"What are you doing?" Laird asked.

"We're going to dance."

I pulled out a *West Side Story* CD, amazed to find it there. "Perfect," I said. I turned on the CD player, stuck in the CD, and forwarded it to the song I wanted. "I Feel Pretty" began, and I took Laird's hands and spun him around, singing along. Soon Laird was singing too, and we were laughing, twirling around and around until we were too dizzy to stand.

"Again!" Laird said when it ended. So we spun and sang, again and again, until I saw Mr. and Mrs. Weinstein standing in the doorway. They were smiling. And before I knew what was happening, they joined us, Mrs. Weinstein graceful in her heels as her husband twirled her around. Laird laughed and jumped up and down, and I took his hand to twirl him too, my mind emptied of anything but this joy.

20

When I got to school Monday, everyone knew about Kyle and me at the movie theater. Girls I sort of knew, girls I used to know really well, and girls I didn't know at all eyed me in the hallway, then turned to each other and whispered. I wanted to kill Claire, but she'd deny it for sure. Missy came up beside me.

"Why do I have to hear from Olivia Hansen that my best friend is going out with Kyle?" she asked.

"We're not going out," I said, striding forward with resolve. "Is that what she's telling people?"

"According to Olivia, you are much less of a prude than your reputation suggests."

"What the hell does that mean?" I glanced up to see Kyle already at his locker, and my heart dropped into my stomach. "Oh God," I said, and I grabbed Missy's arm, steering her back the way we came.

" 'Hell'?" Missy said. She stopped me, holding my arm now. "Did my straight-A, Citizenship Award, ambassador friend just actually say 'hell'? Now I don't know what to believe."

"Missy," I said, laughing now. Thank God for Missy.

"We held hands. We barely even did that. Claire was right there, too."

"You held Kyle's hand in front of Claire and didn't call me immediately?"

"I was going to, I swear." I frowned, remembering the phone call that had distracted me. "Things just got kind of weird at home."

Missy nodded. I didn't have to explain more with her. She knew what my family was like. Even though hers was the closest thing to perfect I'd ever known, she never judged the way my family had turned out.

"So what now?" she asked.

I looked back to see Kyle still digging through his locker. He was so adorable, with his curls hanging into his face. I felt frozen. Surely he'd heard as well that people knew about Saturday. Maybe he regretted holding my hand now.

"Aren't you going to talk to him?" Missy asked, seeing where I was looking. I closed my eyes, trying to think what I should do.

"I don't know," I said finally.

"Linds," Missy said. She held me squarely by the shoulders and waited for me to look at her. "You always do this to yourself. For once, stop worrying about everyone else and do what *you* want."

I sighed. I knew she was right. I got through life moving from one expectation of me to the next. Dad and the premed track, being the good daughter for both Mom and Dad. I did that.

"Okay," I said. "You're right."

I made my way toward Kyle, my mind buzzing, trying to come up with something witty to say. Or I could apologize for moving my locker, which he must have figured out about by now. Or I could mention something about Saturday, the day we held hands. But before any of that could happen, Claire swooped in beside me.

"I have something huge to tell," she said.

"I'm busy," I said, my confidence high. "Anyway, you already told half the school."

"No." She grabbed my arm. "This is different. This is way bigger."

I stopped to face her, keeping an eye on Kyle. I didn't want him to leave before I could talk to him. I wanted to do things differently for once. "Okay," I said. "What's so important?"

"I know the truth about Kyle. The real lowdown."

"What are you talking about?"

"This morning, Kyle told me the reason he moved to New Jersey."

All around us, I could hear people talking and laughing. Lockers slammed and backpacks zipped. I waited.

"He got angry and threw a chair through a window."

"A chair?" I tried to understand. Kyle, with his soft, warm hand, with his brother with Down syndrome, the Kyle I had started to let myself like—this Kyle had been violent? The confidence I had had only moments before began to deflate.

"A few kids got hit with the broken glass and started bleeding, and the teachers didn't want him coming back.

They were scared." Claire paused, searching my face. "He's a bad boy after all."

I set my mouth and willed myself to look toward Kyle. Sam was talking to him now, his hands gesturing.

Missy joined us, looking concerned. "What happened?"

"I knew you'd want to know," Claire said, smiling. She walked off, leaving me there with Missy, people milling around us. I watched as Kyle shut his locker and walked down the hallway toward his first-period class.

"What?" Missy said again. "Didn't you talk to him?"

"We're going to be late," I said.

I walked ahead of her, knowing she hated when I dodged her like that, when I didn't say what was on my mind. But the truth was, I didn't know why it felt like such a big deal. So Kyle had thrown a chair. Why did that seem so much worse than any of the other possibilities? But for some reason, it did. It bothered me terribly, the thought of his lifting that chair like a monster. The strength of his anger as he heaved it across the room. The image was so different from the one that had been forming in my mind since Saturday: a kind person who loved his brother, who maybe had sadness like mine. I didn't like to think there were dark, powerful parts to him rumbling under the surface like a train barreling toward me from far away.

After school, before going into the auditorium, Claire caught me by the arm. I turned, surprised.

"Don't you have rehearsal?" I asked.

"In a few minutes." She gave me one of her smiles that

91

were not really smiles. I looked behind her, afraid Kyle would turn the corner and see me.

"I just wanted to apologize about earlier," she said. "I shouldn't have told Jo about you and Kyle. I assumed she'd know it was private information, but I guess she blurted it to a ton of people." She shook her head so I would know Jo was the one to blame, not her.

"It's not a big deal," I said, too chicken to say what I really thought.

"Have you talked to Kyle?"

That smile of hers crept back onto her face, and I understood. She had known that the information about Kyle would bother me. It was why she insisted on telling me, her way to keep things from progressing between us. I held my mouth shut tight.

"If you want, I can talk to him during rehearsal." She kept her gaze steady. "I can tell him I'm the one who spread the news about your little hand-holding."

"It's fine," I said, hating her for calling it "little." Kyle holding my hand wasn't *little*. I did my best to hold my gaze steady too. "You don't need to say a thing."

Claire gave me a quick, insincere hug and went in to rehearsal. And then Kyle did turn into the hallway. Our eyes met, and he smiled.

"I was wondering when I'd see you," he said.

"Now you can stop wondering. Here I am, in the flesh."

His smile faded at the tone of my voice.

"Is something wrong?"

"Everything's fine," I said. "I just have to get going with my monitoring duties."

I could see the pained look on his face. "Lindsey, why won't you talk to me?" A darkness came over his expression. "Is this because of Zachary?"

"No," I said quickly. "Of course not."

"Then what is it?"

His look was pleading. I considered telling him the truth, that I was upset by his violent outburst at his old school, but I could hear how absurd that would sound. What was so wrong with showing anger? I took a big breath and let it out. "I don't think I'm cut out to be someone's girlfriend," I said finally.

He laughed and shook his head. "That's ridiculous."

"Well," I said seriously, "it's the truth."

I walked away, my heart aching, and when I looked back, he had gone into the auditorium. The door was closing behind him, but while it was still open I could hear the actors' voices echoing off the ceiling as though they were coming from somewhere far away. I dropped to the floor, hating myself. Hating that I couldn't have a normal life with normal girl emotions about a boy. I pulled my bag onto my lap and reached inside. Out came the list of combinations. I turned the dials of three lockers, and stuffed things from them into my bag.

21

First-period Spanish. Missy slid a folded note on her desk over to me, and I shook my head. She knew I tried to pay attention during class, and passing notes was not the way to do that. But she looked at me emphatically and put the note on my desk. When Missy wanted something, few things could stop her. Señora Manuela stood at the board, reviewing gerunds for our test Friday. Her voice was high and singsongy, and I liked the way she trilled her "R"s. I kept my eyes on her but begrudgingly opened the note. It read:

> *Claire is having a party Saturday—only select people invited, including Kyle.*

I glanced at Missy, my throat thick.

So? I mouthed.

But I knew that she meant Claire had purposely orchestrated a gathering from which I would be excluded. She knew my father didn't allow me to go to parties, not since Mark died.

"She's moving in on him," Missy whispered. "You have to do something."

I shook my head and shrugged. "I don't care," I whispered back, but we both knew it was a lie.

That was when Señora Manuela's voice fell silent.

"Señoritas," she said. *"Solamente le preguntare una vez."* I will only ask you once.

I cringed. I couldn't remember the last time a teacher had scolded me. It felt awful to have it happen now, on top of all the other feelings I was experiencing. *"Lo siento,"* I said.

I didn't look at Missy, but I knew exactly what she was thinking. I gave in too easily to Señora Manuela, just like I gave in to Claire and the cruel way she treated me. She was right, of course. I had never stood up to Claire.

Just before class ended, Ms. Keller's receptionist's voice came over the loudspeaker. Emergency school meeting. Everyone was to report to the auditorium before next period.

I glanced at Missy.

"What the hell?" she said as we gathered our things.

I shrugged, but my heart sped up a bit. I already knew.

Ms. Keller stood onstage and made the announcement I expected: A number of students had reported things stolen from their lockers. Everyone needed to be vigilant about protecting their combination. No sharing it with friends. No writing it anywhere.

I listened, feeling dizzy. What did I expect? That no one would care? That no one would get upset, having things taken from them? I closed my eyes, took some deep breaths.

Okay, I thought. Okay.

Calm down now.

There's got to be a way out of this.

But a sinking feeling told me I was wrong.

22

Dad walked beside me as I pushed the cart through the aisles of Costco. His hair looked uncombed, and he was extra quiet—preoccupied, I was sure, with work. I held our list and pointed to things. He pulled them off the shelves and dropped them in the cart.

"That's the wrong brand," I told him when he grabbed a box of Cheerios. Since when did any of us eat Cheerios? He noticed, shook his head, and put it back.

"I've got things on my mind," he said. It was his way of apologizing.

I shrugged and got the Raisin Bran. He often had things on his mind. It hadn't always been like that, though. It hadn't been like that before that client of his killed himself and the family sued Dad. I took a breath, wanting to do things differently for once.

"I think I should be able to go to parties," I said. I didn't look at him, just pushed the cart along.

"Where is this coming from?" I could feel his gaze on me.

"I'm the only person I know who isn't allowed to go to parties."

"You know how I feel about that, Lindsey," he said, as

I knew he would. "Besides, it would get in the way of your schoolwork."

"Mark went wherever he wanted when he was my age." I swallowed. We didn't talk about Mark, especially about when he was my age. The same age when he died.

Dad cleared his throat. He looked intently at a can of soup before putting it back on the shelf. "Things are different now," he said.

I didn't dare say anything else.

We turned the corner to the paper products. I pointed to a pack of paper towels, my chest tight. Maybe I'd try again later.

"How about Tara?" he asked, changing the subject. "Has she been behaving?"

"No more than usual."

He dropped the paper towels into the cart. "I don't know what to do with that girl."

"She needs someone to talk to." I gripped the cart handle, the tightness still there.

Dad walked more briskly. He put a hand into his pocket and loudly shook the change there.

"What are you suggesting?" he said. "That she needs a psychiatrist? I'm a psychiatrist, for God's sake. She can talk to me."

A little girl, standing on the end of a cart, laughed as her mother pushed her.

"That's enough," the woman said. "This isn't safe." The girl frowned, but she climbed off the cart.

I looked away, jealous, as always, of everyone else's normal life.

97

As we neared the end of the next aisle, and as Dad reached for a jar of peanut butter, a display of egg-shaped metal tea infusers caught my eye. Without a thought, I took one and stuffed it into my pants pocket.

That was when I saw her. A young woman with two security guards. She was almost pretty, but completely stony-faced as one of the guards searched inside her purse.

"Whoa," Dad said. "What's happening over there?"

A few other people stopped to watch, and the woman looked down, averting her eyes from all the stares.

"She stole something," I said carefully.

Dad shook his head. "*This* is a person who needs a psychiatrist."

I bit my lip, watching. The guard looking through her purse pulled out something small I couldn't see, and the other guard took a walkie-talkie from his belt and spoke into it. The woman stayed expressionless, her eyes on the floor. Her dark hair hung around her face. A small crowd was gathering now, and I felt light, my heart fluttering, as if it were me getting caught.

With everyone still watching, the guards escorted the woman toward the back of the store.

"Come on." Dad kept moving. "Watching doesn't help anything. She wants the attention."

I pushed the cart, my arms shaky. "What will happen to her?" I asked him.

"Someone will come and bail her out, I imagine." He frowned, still jiggling the coins in his pocket. "Hopefully she'll get the right kind of help."

He continued, talking about impulse control and the

limbic system, but I stopped hearing. I threw items into the cart, lost in my thoughts. Who, I kept wondering, would bail me out if I got seen for who I was?

In my bedroom, I pulled the tea infuser from my pocket, where I'd been aware of it the whole car ride home. I looked at it. What was I going to do with a tea infuser? I took out the shoe box and dropped it in. And I slid the box back under my bed.

23

Dad made his usual toast and jam. He poured himself a cup of coffee and opened the newspaper. I sat across from him, unable to eat.

Today was Halloween, the second anniversary of Mark's death. Dad barely looked up when Tara yelled good-bye and slipped out the door. Tara, who since last year had seen Halloween as an excuse to show skin, was dressed as a stripper. Dad wouldn't have liked that one bit. I, however, was not in costume. It was my way of acknowledging the day's significance. But Dad didn't seem to notice that either. I waited, watching for some sign from him. Finally, I gathered my stuff for school and left.

"Have a nice day," he called after me.

Bite me, I thought.

Half an hour later, I was in the hallway at school. Some kid had a bloody gash on his face. Another had an ax splitting his head. I tried to keep my eyes forward. Otherwise, my mind went places I didn't like. Such as what Mark looked like after the accident. The night it happened, I was trick-or-treating with Tara in our building, so we weren't home when the call came. But Dad found us on the seventh floor. His eyes were wide and wild. He told us Mark was in the hospital and we needed to go with him. I held Tara's hand and she started crying, and we followed Dad to the car. Once we were inside, he put on classical music loud. His hands gripped the wheel and one of his legs was frantically bouncing up and down. Tara kept crying. I closed my eyes and counted backward from one hundred, trying to stay calm.

At the hospital, Mom was in a chair, her body rounded and small, like someone I didn't know. We came closer, and finally she looked up. That was when it was clear. It was too late. He hadn't survived. My father bent to his knees and held my mother. It was the last time I would see them hug. It was also when I first understood I couldn't break down as well. I had to stay strong because if I didn't, who would?

I snapped myself back now. I didn't want to travel down that road, especially not today. Missy stood by her locker, and I made my way over.

"How are you holding up?" she asked. She, of course, remembered what today was. She was wearing a T-shirt that said SHOOT ME IF I SAY HELLA. This wasn't a costume. She never dressed up either, but not for the same reason as me. She just thought the whole thing was ridiculous.

"I'll live."

She grabbed my hand. "Halloween sucks all the way around. Let's just get through the day."

I smiled. I honestly didn't know what I would have done without Missy. I kept an eye out for Kyle. We hadn't spoken since crossing paths outside the auditorium, but he was still everywhere—in the hallways, by the bus stop, on the sidewalks of my neighborhood. I knew it was my fault, saying what I did, but I hated that he believed me, that he hadn't come after me, like in all those Hollywood love stories.

"Are you coming over later to hand out candy?" I asked Missy, trying to think of something else. It was what we'd done the year after Mark died. She knew I didn't want to be alone.

"Of course." She ran a finger through her hair, which I noticed she'd been wearing down lately. "But I'm going to be a little late."

"Why?"

"I have something I have to do."

"That's mysterious," I said. "What's happening?"

Before she could respond, Sam popped up behind her, wearing a George Bush mask.

Missy laughed. "Now, that's frightening."

Sam laughed too and took off the mask.

"Whoa," he said when he saw me. "Why don't you take the mask off before you scare the crap out of everyone?" He laughed again briefly. But then he shuffled his feet, standing close to Missy. Not Sam-like at all. Missy smiled at him and didn't say anything about his lame joke. Not Missy-like either. After a beat, Sam said good-bye and walked on.

"What in the world was that about?" I frowned at Missy.

"What?"

"Don't be coy with me." Then a lightbulb went off. "No. It can't be true."

"I was going to tell you, Linds." Missy adjusted her

backpack. "I don't want everyone making a big deal out of it."

"Sam?" I said, still flabbergasted. "Our Sam?"

"You don't know what he's like when it's just him and me. He's actually thoughtful and says the nicest things." She giggled a little.

"No," I said again. "You can't giggle. My Missy doesn't giggle."

"Last night, he told me my hands were like delicate flowers." She looked at her hands, clearly remembering.

"Get out of here!" I yelled.

Missy covered my mouth with her hand and glanced down the hallway. "Do not tell anyone. You have to promise. It's new. I want to see where it goes before everyone knows."

I shook my head. "I may block it from my mind entirely." Really, though, I was impressed. Missy went after what she wanted, no matter what anyone else thought.

"Good." She smiled at me. "Nothing's happened yet, but he invited me over after school."

"This is why you'll be late? Because you'll be kissing Sam?"

"Keep your voice down, Linds. I mean it." She said it harshly and quietly, like the Missy I knew, and I laughed.

"Thank you," I told her.

"For what?"

"For taking my mind completely off my own life."

She took my arm and we made our way down the hall. "Anytime."

* * *

During second period, Ms. Keller's receptionist came to the classroom door. She whispered something to the teacher, and then she motioned to me.

Oh God.

This was it.

I followed her down the hallway toward Ms. Keller's office, my mind racing, trying to think of what I would say.

Ms. Keller waved at me.

"Come on in," she said. "Have a seat."

She stood to close the door. I squeezed my hands in my lap. They were soaked with sweat.

"I wanted to hear from you," she started as she sat behind her desk, "because you were the first one to have something stolen."

I held perfectly still. "I was?"

"You changed lockers because of it." She bent her head, concerned. "Didn't you?"

I swallowed. Ms. Keller had always been so nice to me. She'd been really patient after Mark died, and then she'd trusted me to be the tenth-grade ambassador. She didn't deserve my lies.

"That's right," I said.

"What was it that was stolen?"

I waited, trying to come up with something credible. The heater clicked on, and a whirring began.

"I'm putting together a list, for the police," she explained.

I swallowed again, my heart thumping.

104

"It was nothing," I said quickly. "A pencil."

"A pencil?"

Of all the stupid things to come up with. But it was too late to change my answer, so I nodded.

Ms. Keller watched me, obviously confused. She scribbled something on a pad, then stood and opened her door.

"Okay," she said. "You can go back to class."

I got up slowly and walked toward the door. At the threshold, I hesitated and turned. Ms. Keller had opened a drawer, busy with something. I wanted to confess. I wanted for this to be over with, for something to change.

"Ms. Keller?" I said.

She looked up, her eyes distracted. "Yes?"

I shook my head, my nerve gone.

"Nothing," I said, and walked out.

24

I turned on some music, and Laird came over to Sol and me and we danced around the family room, laughing. Sometimes I loved my babysitting job just for the way it pulled me from my own life, let me be in the moment the way small children always are.

Laird stopped spinning. "I smell something."

I sniffed the air, then Sol's butt. "You're right," I said. "We'll be right back."

I took Sol up to his parents' room, where his changing table was. The bedroom was light and spacious. A large square of sun angled onto the carpet from a skylight. The huge bed was made, pillows fluffed at the top. I laid Sol on his table and was bending to get a fresh diaper when something on the dresser caught my eye.

Money. A big wad of bills. Twenty-dollar bills, to be exact. Next to it was a ruby necklace and matching bracelet.

That familiar feeling rose up. A tension starting in my chest, moving slowly toward my throat, where it lodged, feeling like a cry.

Sol babbled, his legs kicking.

"I'm coming, little man," I said softly. I got the diaper and got busy taking off his dirty one. No, I told myself. Not from the Weinsteins, who trusted me to take care of their children. Who trusted me so much that they could leave money lying around. Who does that unless it doesn't even cross their mind that someone—that I—might think about taking it? The last thing I wanted was to mess that up. I loved this job. That tightness in my throat was still there, but I pushed through it, fastening Sol's diaper and taking him out of the room. I closed the door behind us, and pulled it shut as tightly as I could.

25

Claire smiled from across the table.

"What, Claire?"

"Don't pretend you don't know." She turned to Jo, who smiled an equally evil smile. Was there some mean-girls class where they'd learned to perfect their smiles?

"I don't know." I took a bite of my sandwich, wanting Missy there with me. She was helping Mr. Little, the science teacher, compile research for the project they were submitting to some regional conference.

"About Missy."

Uh-oh.

"And Sam."

I picked the caraway seeds out of my bread, trying to look detached. "I don't know what you're talking about."

"They're dating," Jo said.

I shrugged. "So what?"

Claire cut her eyes at me. I could see Kyle in the cafeteria line, nodding at some guy behind him. I looked back at my sandwich, wishing I hadn't looked up.

"So," Claire said, "they're odd couple of the year."

"People can't help who they choose."

As soon as it was out of my mouth, I knew it was a

108

mistake. "Are you talking about you and Kyle?" she said, her expression even.

"There is no me and Kyle."

"Because you recognize you have nothing in common." She tossed her hair behind her shoulder. "Unlike some people we know."

"Yeah." Jo nodded, the bobblehead in action. "You were smart. Now, Missy and Sam . . ."

I looked at them. They were the ones I was nothing like, but I didn't have the guts to say it. Instead I said, "Kyle and I aren't that different." I held my gaze steady as Claire's expression turned to surprise. Only now, after saying it, did I think it was probably true. I knew what it was like to feel angry. I was feeling it now, just looking at Claire and Jo.

I put down my sandwich, my appetite gone. I didn't have to sit there and take Claire's crap. Why had I been caring so long what she thought of me? Missy was right: Claire was the one who was jealous of me. Yet I had allowed her to turn that around for so long, making it look as if I was the jealous one. For whatever reason, it was all coming clear now, like when a fog lifts and suddenly the sky is bright blue. I had never been jealous of Claire. There was nothing to be jealous of. She was mean and heartless, and she had never been my friend. I stood and picked up my tray. "See you guys later."

I walked over to the bus tub, getting there just as Kyle left the line.

"Hey," I said to him.

"You're talking to me now?" he asked.

"I didn't stop talking to you. You stopped talking to me."

"Don't turn this around," he said. "You basically told me to go away, so I did."

I bit my lip. How had I so royally screwed this up? How had I taken the one thing that had made me happy since Mark died and turned it into a mess? "I don't want you to go away," I said softly.

"What *do* you want, then?" he asked.

I glanced over at Claire, who was watching our conversation intently. Kyle's question was big. It was the eight-million-dollar question. What did I want? I wanted so much, so much that I didn't have, so much I had lost, that I couldn't begin to know how to answer. So I said simply: "I don't know."

He shook his head, frustrated. "Let me know when you do."

I watched him walk off, my heart in my throat. I couldn't have felt more alone as I wove past the other kids, all joking and chatting, and went out into the hallway. There, just twenty feet away, Ms. Keller was speaking with two policemen in front of a row of lockers. I turned quickly and walked in the other direction.

26

A few afternoons later, I brought Dad a glass of water and aspirin and gave his shoulders a few rubs. He was sitting at the computer. He patted my hand, which meant he expected me to be in my good-daughter mode. So I struck.

"Remember I asked you about parties?" I started, feeling brave after what had happened with Claire and Jo.

"Hmm."

"It's not just parties. It's other stuff too." I rested my hands on his shoulders and spoke fast now so he wouldn't have time to think too much. "Like dating."

"Lindsey, we've been over this before."

"But life is more than just school, Dad." I tried to keep my voice even, but inside I felt as if I were going to explode. Just one thing, I thought. Just let me have one thing.

He rubbed his face, his old familiar gesture, and I let my hands fall to my sides, waiting. Knowing already how hopeless it was. He turned and looked at me.

"Please, Lindsey," he said. "I have reports to write up. I have two patients later this evening. Your sister is out of control." His eyes were watery and old. "I need you to not do this."

I closed my eyes, squeezing against tears. I understood. It was the same as always. I should have been furious. I should have let him know once and for all what it felt like to have to fit inside his lines, to never deviate from the person he wanted me to be. I should have yelled at him about Claire and how I had allowed her to treat me. How I had let Kyle slip from my hands. Maybe I should have even picked up a chair and thrown it across the room. But instead I went to my room, still the good daughter. The daughter who had to make up for his loss.

27

Dad and Tara were fighting again. Their fighting had increased last year too when we got closer to our December visit with Mom. This time, I sat in my room, my headphones on, singing softly. I didn't want to get involved. But I could still make out some words—"last time" and "regret" and "alone." I tried not to listen.

Eventually, there was a knock at my door. I opened it, and Dad stood on the other side.

"I'm going out of town," he announced. He leaned against the doorjamb and ran a hand through his hair.

"Again?" I tried to control the frustration in my voice.

"It's a drug conference in Denver." He frowned. "Tara needs someone around more. But I have to attend these conferences. I need to build up my name again." He meant since the malpractice suit. I didn't say anything. He didn't usually mention the suit, so when he did, I didn't know how best to respond. I would've liked to tell him he was right about Tara. We both needed someone around more. But I knew saying so would only stress him out further.

"Fine." I pushed past him into the hallway. Tara came out of her room at the same time. She pointed at me again, reminding me that I was hers. But I didn't care if she thought she had something on me. It was clear Dad would always see things the way he did: Tara was the bad one and I was the good one. And he was the one who made sure everything appeared just fine.

"What are you going to do about it?" Missy asked, referring to Claire's recent announcement that Kyle now came regularly to her house to help her with lines. The play's opening night was a few weeks off. We were walking to lunch. On a bunch of lockers, someone had posted drawings of a stick figure wearing a hat and scarf, with a pencil and book in its hands. WANTED DEAD OR ALIVE, it said. BCD LOCKER THIEF.

Very funny.

Those posters would be down by next period. Ms. Keller did not find the situation funny at all.

"There's nothing I can do," I said. "Claire does what she wants."

"You can talk to Kyle," Missy said. "You know, make more of an effort."

"I'm working on it." I pushed the cafeteria doors open.

Missy gestured toward the table where Claire sat talking with Kyle. "You better work faster."

I'd planned on writing off Claire for good, but Missy was right. I couldn't just walk away and let Claire swoop up Kyle. I took a deep breath as we approached them.

"Hello, girls," Claire said, making us sound young and stupid. "Kyle and I were just talking about the play."

Kyle looked at me unhappily.

I smiled at Claire, then at Kyle. "Maybe you want to be

114

alone," I said, looking at Kyle. The tension between us was thick enough to slice. He let out a little noise, letting me know he was annoyed.

"Actually," Claire said in her best apologetic voice, "that would be good. It's not like you two are a part of the play."

Missy shook her head. "Believe me," she said, "we don't want to sit here." She took my arm and swept me away. I didn't have time to see Kyle's reaction.

After last period, I sat in the hallway during rehearsal, my hands tucked beneath my legs. I wasn't going to be doing any more locker stealing. That was for sure.

Instead of going home, I took the 44 bus to the mall. I didn't feel like seeing Kyle. I didn't want to go home, where Dad and Tara were surely fighting. I just wanted to stop thinking for once. I wanted everything to go away.

The mall was busy. Christmas music tinkled down from the ceiling. Tables filled with stocking stuffers—lip glosses, ornaments, stickers, glass figurines, books full of quotes to enhance your life—stood unmanned outside stores. I needed none of it. Didn't want any of it. But I took a few things anyway.

At home, I dropped it all in the box. I didn't know what I planned to do with this stuff. Mostly, I didn't want to look at it again, packaged and new, a reminder of what I couldn't seem to stop.

As I lay in bed that night, I swore I could feel the stolen goods under there—bulging, pulsing—very much like in the story about the princess and the pea. And so I stayed awake.

28

Two days before we left for Mom's and the evening before the play's opening night, I stood in the Weinsteins' kitchen while Mrs. Weinstein rushed around, pouring milk for Laird, pulling out applesauce for Sol. She wore a green velvet dress, heels, and a slim-fitting black overcoat. She and Mr. Weinstein were going to a holiday party.

"Let me," I said. I took the applesauce from her and got out Sol's bowl and spoon. The boys were playing in the living room. "Just go. Have fun."

"I don't know what we would do without you," she said. She smiled, and then, without warning, she came across the room and hugged me. The smell of her perfume wafted around me, and her thin arms were warm around my back. I held still, surprised. I hadn't been hugged in a long time. When she pulled away, I looked at the floor, overwhelmed by her warmth. By her open expression of affection. She didn't notice, just picked up a small package from the counter and handed it to me.

"No," I said. "I can't."

"Oh, please. Don't be so polite. Just open it."

I undid the tape and folded back the paper. Inside was

a *West Side Story* CD. My eyes filled and I put a hand over my mouth.

"For you," Mrs. Weinstein said, still smiling.

I shook my head. "I don't know what to say."

"You don't have to say anything. Consider it your Christmas bonus." And before I could say anything else, she leaned out of the kitchen and called upstairs, "Jack. Let's go."

Opening night. Sam, Missy, and I came up the walkway to the school. That day, the first snow of the season had fallen. It clung thinly to the dead trees and grass. The school was beginning to take on its picturesque quality, the one captured in its brochures. Icicles hanging off the eaves. Snow clinging to the brick, the trees lush and soft with the white weight of it. As much as I felt displaced here, as much as I disliked that the kids wore Gucci and Prada while the teachers drove to school in used Hondas, and as much as I hated that no one ever said anything about any of it, the campus was really pretty.

The three of us sat in the first mezzanine. The room was full of parents, students, and teachers. Near the front of the auditorium, I could make out Claire's parents. Her mother's fur was hung over the back of her chair. Jewelry glistened in her ears and at her neck. Claire's father sat beside her in a jacket and tie. They were both smiling. I felt the familiar disappointment. It could have been my parents—or at least my father—sitting there and grinning with pride.

The lights dimmed and Missy nudged me as the

curtains opened. Our classmates sang "Oh, What a Beautiful Mornin'," and I couldn't help but mouth the words under my breath. I knew Claire was backstage, getting ready for her first scene. I tried not to let my disappointment ruin the night.

Missy and Sam held hands next to me. Their relationship was no longer secret, and after an initial buzz, most of the sophomore class had quieted down. Missy was happy in a way I had never seen before. She was less militant, sweeter. Not that she had lost her edge. She was currently gathering signatures to get some acknowledgment of Hanukkah and Kwanzaa in classrooms during the holiday season. I was happy for her. But I couldn't help that this was another reason to feel sad tonight. It wasn't that long ago that Kyle had been holding my hand in a dark theater.

After a standing ovation, we joined the crowd in the hallway. All the parents were talking and laughing and congratulating each other on their sons' and daughters' performances. On the walls, someone had hung signs for auditions for the spring play, *West Side Story*.

"It's your favorite," Missy said when she saw me looking. "I hope you try out for this one."

I frowned. I wanted this so badly. But if it came out that I was the locker thief, my ambassador days would be over. All my days at BCD might be over, for all I knew.

"I don't know," I said finally. "I'd like to, but . . ."

Missy looked up at Sam. "You should hear her sing. She's gifted."

"Is that so?" Sam said. "Sing us a little something."

"Very funny," I told him.

"What, too crowded?" he went on. "Pretend you're alone, in the shower. You can start by taking off your clothes."

Missy glared at him. "You did not just say that in front of me."

Sam went pale. "I'm sorry, Miss."

"What is wrong with you?" she said. "You're like a subspecies."

"I'm sorry," he said again. This wasn't the first time I had seen them like this. Regardless of Missy's stories about the sweet things they said to one another in private, Missy was still Missy, and Sam, for all his attempts at self-control, was still Sam.

Missy kicked him in the shin, not so hard as to attract attention but hard enough to make him bend over and rub his leg.

"Sorry, Lindsey," Missy said, and she stormed off.

"Wait." Sam hobbled after her.

I watched them go, shaking my head. That was when I saw Kyle. He wore a knit cap and a red scarf, and he was going out through the main doors. I knew if I thought about it too long, I would lose my nerve, so I pushed my way through the crowd.

Outside, the lights in front of the school made the snow glisten. Kyle was halfway down the walk, heading toward a car idling at the curb. His family, I guessed.

"Kyle," I called. "Wait up!"

He turned, and seeing me there, he waited as I trotted to catch up. I stopped before him. Our breath was visible in the cold. His cheeks were slightly rosy, his lips full and inviting.

119

"The play was really good," I said.

"You think?"

I nodded. "Really, really good."

A beat of silence passed, and I took a breath. "Listen, I want to apologize. For being rude. For everything."

He waited. "I'm listening," he said.

"I do know what I want. I want to be with you."

He didn't respond.

"I got scared."

"Scared," he said. He was making this so hard. But I had to speak my mind.

"It's just—just that I've never liked anyone like this before."

He kept watching me, and my face felt flushed. I didn't know what he was thinking, but I plodded on. "And when I heard the reason you came to New Jersey, I freaked out."

"Because I got in trouble at my old school?"

I nodded. "I know it sounds weird. I should have talked to you."

"Lindsey," he said. "A kid made fun of my brother. I got angry. What's the big deal?"

I blinked, understanding now. He had thrown that chair in defense of his brother.

"I was envious," I blurted. As soon as I said it, I knew it was true. I wanted to be able to get angry the way he had. That was why it bothered me so much. It wasn't that Kyle was "bad" and I was "good," like Claire had tried to convince me. We were the same. I was just too afraid to see it. I opened my mouth, wanting to say more, wanting to explain better.

"You're a weird girl," Kyle said, and laughed.

I nodded, figuring this was it. I had exposed myself, after all. It was what I had been afraid of doing all along.

"My family's waiting," he said, gesturing to the car. I looked over at the Jeep Cherokee. Zachary, I imagined, was inside. My stomach felt empty as I remembered that day at the movies. "Listen," he said then. "Maybe we could get together soon and talk more."

I nodded, my heart suddenly filling. "I'm leaving for California tomorrow. I'll be back in two weeks."

"In two weeks, then." He leaned forward and, to my surprise, kissed me on the cheek. His face was warm, his lips soft. No boy had ever kissed me before.

I smiled.

No, I beamed.

As I watched him walk to the car, happiness coursed through my body. I waved at the car, unable to contain myself. And I touched my cheek lightly with my fingertips. It was happening, maybe: Kyle and me. And the best part was that I had made it happen, simply by being me.

When I turned back, Claire stood on the stoop outside the building with her parents. She still had on heavy makeup from the play, and she held a few dozen roses in her arms. Her parents were talking, but she was watching me.

She had seen.

I grinned. She didn't know that she no longer mattered to me. I didn't give a rip about what she thought. And now that I was high on Kyle's kiss, I couldn't help myself. I felt empowered, maybe for the first time ever. I looked right at her and, with that grin still on my face, I yelled: "Ha!"

29

Mom stood on the other side of Security, her hands together, a worried look on her face. She wore a long coat that was lined with fur. Something, I assumed, she'd bought with money from her new husband, Dave. I spotted her before she saw Tara and me, and I could tell by her expression she wasn't simply worried about whether we'd made it onto the airplane. She was worried about the whole next two weeks together. I didn't blame her. I was feeling the same way. Tara, who had tried to convince Dad the night before that she was terrified of flying so she wouldn't have to come, had sat quietly beside me the whole six-hour trip, her iPod in her ears and her eyes stuck on a *Seventeen*. I'd read a book from my AP English class but was unable to focus. My thoughts were too busy with everything else: Mom and her new family, and especially Kyle, who I would see when I returned.

Mom saw us, and her expression changed to delight—feigned delight. I had seen how she really felt.

"My girls!" she gushed.

I hugged her and inhaled her familiar perfume. Maybe this wouldn't be so bad. Maybe it would be a good thing to be together again, even with Dave and his son, Cooper, there. When she hugged Tara, Tara looked at me over Mom's shoulder as if she wanted to kill me. What exactly *I* had done, I didn't know.

On the ride to her house, Mom filled the air with talk about what she had planned. Shopping and dinners and a party on Christmas Eve. When I glanced into the backseat, I noticed that Tara had her iPod in again. The landscape outside turned from billboards and factories spouting smoke to old apartment buildings, then to houses here and there. We pulled off an exit, and soon big, Spanish-style stucco homes with red-tiled roofs and fruit trees clustered along the road. Mom slowed as she turned into one of the driveways. I wasn't surprised that Mom had wound up with this again—a big house and a nice car. It was how things had been with Dad too, before we had had to move.

Tara and I followed her inside.

"We're here!" she called in a singsongy voice as soon as we stepped into the foyer. Mom took our bags from us and dropped them at the bottom of the stairs. The walls in the foyer were stylishly painted a deep, rich burgundy, and a chandelier hung from a high ceiling. Mom set her hand on the dark-wood banister, which curved up and out of sight. I noticed a new ring on her hand, a diamond as big as a pea.

"I'll take you to your room later," she said. "First I want you to see everyone. You won't believe how big Cooper is."

Tara rolled her eyes. "Like we care," she mumbled.

I nudged her, hoping Mom hadn't heard. But Mom was in a flurry of activity, running from doorway to doorway, looking for Cooper and Dave. Dave emerged, a dish towel in his hands. He was tall and thin and wore a beard that was sprinkled with gray. He was some kind of doctor. Not a psychiatrist, but something having to do with the brain, or the skull, or something like that.

"Lindsey, Tara." He smiled. "Nice to see you again."

He gripped the towel in his hands, clearly as uncomfortable as we were. How does one greet the daughters of the woman who chose you and your son over them?

"We're happy to be here," I said. I glanced at Tara, who nodded at him. I glared at her, hoping she'd look at me. I wanted her to be pleasant, to not make this any worse than it had to be. Especially for Dave. He hadn't done anything wrong. But she didn't turn her head.

"Where's Cooper?" Mom asked. That smile was still pasted to her face.

"Cooper," Dave called sternly up the stairs. "Get down here."

There was some rustling and then some floorboards creaked, and Cooper descended the stairs. Mom had been right. He was completely different than when we had seen him last year. A foot taller, and thinner. His hair was short and stood up in little spikes.

"Hi," he said, and shrugged.

"Hi." I smiled. I didn't want him to feel uncomfortable too.

Later, after Mom had shown us to the guest room and we were unpacking our things, Tara started in on me.

"This is bullshit," she said.

"What is?" I refolded the sweater that was in my hands.

"You know what." She sat on the bed and looked out the window. "Mom and Dave and Cooper. This whole thing."

"Look, Tara." I sat on the bed across from her. "Mom got remarried. She's entitled to do that."

Tara looked at me blankly. "That's not what I mean, and you know it."

I supposed I did know. She meant Mom's convenient denial about the real reason she had moved so far away, far from the memories Tara and I represented. I wanted to agree, to tell Tara I felt left behind and discarded too. As if I meant nothing to Mom. But if I acknowledged my feelings, if I allowed myself to wade in the anger Tara was drenched in, what would happen? Who would make things easier, give Mom a reason to keep us in her life at all? I might have come to an understanding about my fears, but it didn't mean I was ready to act on that, to make so many changes so quickly.

"Tara," I said. "Don't make this worse than it has to be."

Tara gave me a look and promptly left the room.

30

Christmas morning, we opened presents. As always, Mom doled out each wrapped gift, one at a time. It was her way of keeping everything in order and under control. Tara rolled her eyes at me. She checked her watch, no doubt calculating what time it was back in New Jersey and whether she could catch one of her friends on the phone. Cooper unwrapped a new baseball glove. Tara unwrapped a blue cashmere scarf-and-glove set. I unwrapped the same set in red.

Afterward, we gave our obligatory thank-yous and Mom and Dave wandered off to labor over the Christmas dinner. Tara rushed straight to the phone, and Cooper tromped upstairs to his bedroom to play with new toys. I went upstairs, something nagging at me that I couldn't identify. I walked through the hallway, stopping to look at the pictures hanging there: baby pictures of Cooper, wedding photos, and one of Tara and me from a few years ago. There were none of Mark. I peered into the master bedroom. The bed was made with a silky cream comforter. A chaise stood against the wall across from the bed. The dresser top was barren except for a small glass jewelry box I recognized, the same one Mom had had when she'd lived with us. It was the only thing I had seen in this house that was from that time. I went in and put my hand on it, felt its smooth, cool shape beneath my palm. I lifted the top. Inside were necklaces, pins, and bracelets I didn't recognize, all probably bought with Dave's money to fill Mom's new life. I sifted through them, feeling the gold chains slide through my fingers. Beneath one of the pins, a pair of diamond drop earrings winked up at me. Earrings I knew. Earrings Dad had bought her for their anniversary the year before Mark died. I grasped them, a feeling rising to my throat. I knew then what was bothering me. It was those cashmere sets Mom had given us. So different from the Weinsteins' gift. The CD referred to something special. But the scarf and gloves were generic—two things without meaning. Two sets in different colors, something you would get an acquaintance. She didn't know who Tara and I were anymore.

I closed my fist over the earrings, shut the lid, and went quickly to the guest room, where I dropped them into my bag. One, two. Two pieces of my mother to take back home.

31

"Who's the guy?" Tara asked me as she browsed through an after-Christmas sale in a Berkeley boutique.

I turned to her, surprised. I had been looking out the window, not shopping at all. Tara, meanwhile, had amassed a good few items to take into the dressing room. Our mother was down the street, getting Cooper a hot chocolate from a coffee shop, but she would be back soon. "What are you talking about?"

"Please." Tara ran her hand over a sequined sweater, checked its size. "I know that look. Every girl I know has gotten it at least once."

"Tara," I said. "You don't know anything. You're thirteen."

She looked at me, unfazed. "Who is it?"

I sighed and joined her in looking at sweaters. The truth was, I did want to talk about Kyle. He had been on my mind almost constantly since we'd left. "He's new this year."

"Kyle Torren."

I looked at her. "You know him?"

"Hello," she said. "Any girl with eyes knows who he is." She smiled. "I didn't think you went for bad boys."

"He's not a bad boy."

She shrugged. "That's not what I heard."

"Well," I said, snatching a sweater from her hand, "you heard wrong. Don't you think you're trying on enough clothes?"

She watched me, but I avoided her eyes. "I'm not buying it anymore, you know," she said.

"What are you talking about?" I moved to another rack, but she followed.

"The credit card, the bad boy. What else are you hiding?"

"God, Tara," I said. "Why can't you just leave it alone?"

Now her voice grew thin and sharp, full of rage. In a less public setting, she might have started yelling. "Because," she said, "don't you get it? As long as you play the good girl, I always get pegged as the bad one."

"That's not true," I said, trying to calm her, though inside I could feel my own anxiety rising.

"It is too. Why can't you just admit it?"

"You're acting crazy," I said, still working to keep my voice steady.

She walked away and threw the clothes she had been carrying on the counter, where a saleswoman was putting tags on garments. "I don't want these," she barked at the woman, who startled and looked up. Tara passed me as she headed for the door. "You're the most selfish person in the world," she said.

I turned back to the saleswoman. "I'm sorry. She's having a bad day."

"Happens to the best of us," the woman said.

I smiled, but inside I was roiling. Tara's words were

ringing through my head. How dare she call me selfish? Me, the one who held everything together. The one who walked carefully away from her own desires so that Tara and everyone else could have what they wanted. I opened the door and stepped onto the sidewalk. I saw her heading in the direction of the coffee shop where our mother had said she'd be.

I felt as if I might cry. Or else burst, my guts splattering onto the concrete. Everyone would finally get to see what was inside me. I wished I could talk to Kyle right then. I wished I could hold his warm hand.

A few pigeons pecked at an empty wrapper on the street. They pushed it around a bit, then left it smashed against the curb.

What, I wondered, was inside me? Really inside me? If I felt like crying, why couldn't I just cry?

Back at Mom's house, I dialed Kyle's number, but the voice mail answered. I tried Missy instead.

"How is it out there?" she asked.

"It's complete and utter hell. Worse than last year."

I looked out the window of the bedroom. Birds flitted between orange trees, and flowers were in bloom. Flowers in December. What was I doing here?

"Well," Missy said, "I hope you're coming back sooner than later, and not just because things suck there. The drama's increasing here."

"What's going on?"

"Claire's working double-time on Kyle with you out of town."

I froze. Immediately, I remembered my "Ha!" What a stupid thing to do. Claire was definitely looking for payback.

"Missy," I said. "You have to stop her."

"Stop the Claire machine?"

I put my head in my hands. I was screwed.

32

A week later, Tara and I pulled up in a taxi outside our apartment. Dad had known he'd be working, so he had given us the money to get home. Tara had barely spoken to me since that day in the store, and she took off ahead of me now as I paid the cabdriver. I was a panicky mess. I thought of Kyle as the driver yanked our bags from the trunk. I just wanted to talk to him, to know that he was waiting for me.

By the time I got to our apartment, Tara's door was already closed, loud music muffled behind it. On the hallway console, I spotted a fruit basket, a big one. I walked over to look at it: apples, oranges, salamis, cheeses. The Fannos had gone all out this year. Near the back was the envelope I was looking for. I slid it out and opened it:

> *Wishing you peace this holiday season.*
> *All our best,*
> *the Fannos*

Some people would have given up by now. After two years of gifts and cards and no response. I had to give them that.

I took the card to my room, where I put it in the drawer

with the others. Then I dragged my bag in there too. I lay back on my bed. It was good to be home, to be able to just lie there, not having to think about whatever event Mom had planned next. The two weeks had been packed with outings, Mom's way to keep the reality of the situation— her daughters visiting her in her new life that didn't include them—at bay. It was easier here, where Dad dealt by not being around at all.

The phone rang, and I went to the hallway to get it.

"Where have you been?" said the voice.

"Claire?"

"I've been trying to reach you for days."

"I was in California," I said. I went to my room and closed the door. There was only one reason Claire would be calling after everything that had happened.

"I want you to hear this from me, Lindsey. Not someone else."

I gripped the phone and walked to the window. "Go ahead."

"It's Kyle. Kyle and me," she said. My throat tightened at the sound of his name. "He kissed me." I heard the sound of my father coming through the front door, the shuffle of his feet as he opened the hall closet to hang up his coat and scarf. I closed my eyes. "I'm sorry, but it's what happened," Claire went on. "I hope you won't hate me."

"I can't talk right now," I said.

"Lindsey—" Claire started, but I hung up. I held the phone in my hand, my breath coming fast. Everything was ruined again. It was what I got, I guessed, for thinking that Kyle wanted us to be together and, of course, for doing the worst thing of all—acting like I'd one-upped the almighty Claire. It was what I got for thinking my life would ever be something worthwhile again after Mark died.

I zipped open my suitcase to put away my clothes. As I pulled out a striped sweater, those diamond earrings fell onto the floor. I picked them up and went to the mirror, where I put them on. I turned my head from side to side, watching them glitter against my face, making me look glamorous. Making me look important.

That was when Dad knocked and opened the door.

"Welcome home," he said.

I turned to face him, the earrings like weights in my ears. The earrings he had given Mom ages ago now. I didn't want him to think she had passed them on to me. But I certainly didn't want him to know the truth. "Thanks," I said.

"Flight was okay?"

"Fine." I held still, waiting.

"Well, then. We'll order Chinese for dinner."

I nodded. He smiled, and I watched as he pulled the door shut. He hadn't even noticed. And something about that—something about the way his obliviousness proved that I was just as invisible as I felt inside—gave me the impetus to do what I did next.

33

The Weinsteins' bedroom was dark, so I flipped on a light. As usual, their bed was made. Vacuum lines marked the pale carpet. I slipped off my shoes and tiptoed to the dresser. I looked along its length, but there was no money. It was spotless except for a single pair of cuff links. I picked them up and examined them. They were gold, the letters "JW" engraved on their flat surfaces. Jack Weinstein. I rubbed the letters with my thumb, my stomach hollow, and I dropped them into my pocket.

A song started on Laird's video downstairs. The baby was napping. I could have felt bad then.

I should have.

But I only felt an adrenaline rush, a filling in of those empty spaces inside. And with it, the acute sense that I could be caught. It was like having a camera focused right on me and waiting for the *click*.

What I wanted, really, was for someone to find me here, undone.

Later, when they got back, Mrs. Weinstein urged her husband to drive me home because of the cold weather.

"Did you have a nice holiday?" he asked once we were on our way.

"Yes, thank you." The cold of the leather seat seeped through my jeans into my legs.

"Most people hate this time of year, but I love it." He turned to smile at me. "They focus on the crowds and the hassles. Why not focus on the good stuff? Like the lights and good food and the kids."

I smiled back at him, remembering how he'd danced with his wife that afternoon in their living room.

His cuff links dug into my thigh, and I looked out the window. Maybe Tara was right. Maybe I was just a selfish person beneath it all. Light snow had begun to fall, just barely dusting the sidewalks. I often complained that everything had been taken from me, but I took what I wanted.

After Mr. Weinstein dropped me off, I went into my room and took the cuff links out of my pocket. I shook them around in my hand, my palms damp, then pulled out the box under my bed. I dropped them into the box and quickly put back the lid, not wanting to see.

34

Monday, back at school, I kept my head down. I didn't want to see anybody. Not Kyle, not Claire. Not even Missy, who thought I was better than I was. I tucked my books against my chest, wishing I had just stayed home. But home was no better. At least here I could lose myself in my classes, keep my mind off everything else.

But between second and third periods, Kyle came up behind me.

"Welcome back. How was California?"

I winced. "It was fine. How were things here?" I tried to sound as light as possible, not wanting him to think I cared.

"Boring," he said.

"That's not what I heard."

He frowned. "What did you hear?"

He watched me, waiting. But Claire walked up, as though she had directed the moment herself.

"I told her," she said to Kyle, flipping back her hair. "About the kiss."

Kyle's face contorted and turned red. He stammered. So it was true. I turned and walked away quickly.

"Lindsey!" Kyle came after me. "That's not what happened."

I faced him. A group of girls who were gathered around a locker turned to see what was going on. "It doesn't matter," I said. "You don't owe me anything."

"It does matter. She threw herself at me."

I eyed him, wanting to believe him, but Claire didn't throw herself on anyone. She didn't have to.

"I doubt that," I told him.

"It's true," he said. His eyes were wild. "She had a cast party, and she caught me alone when I was waiting for the bathroom. She was just talking, and then all of a sudden she was kissing me. I pushed her off right away."

I shook my head, hating the thought of them kissing, even for a moment. "Every boy at this school wants Claire to kiss him like that," I said.

He held his hands open as though he were offering something. "Not me. Don't you get that yet?"

"I don't believe you."

He frowned and shook his head. "Then you are definitely not as smart as you say you are."

I kept my eyes on his, my gaze solid and challenging, but inside I felt weak.

"After everything that's happened, do you really think I would choose Claire over you?"

He waited, but I stayed silent.

"We're the same, Lindsey." He pointed at my heart and then his own. "You and me are the same."

I took a breath. I wanted to believe him. I did. But I just didn't know. Claire was beautiful and charming. And I was just a phony. A thief and a liar. The best student in the sophomore class.

Before I could answer, he shook his head. Then he turned away and thwacked a locker with his open hand. The sound rang through the hall. The girls watching stepped back, away from his line of fire and from his purposeful strides toward the stairs. Claire stood watching too.

Then she met my eyes.

Seeing her there, I felt anger rise to my throat. She had set this whole thing up, just to push me to the sidelines once again.

Everyone was silent, waiting to see what I would do.

"Stay the hell away from me," I told her.

Someone gasped.

A couple of girls covered their mouths.

Claire cut her eyes at me. "You don't talk to me like that."

I didn't budge. "I just did."

She pressed her lips together. "You'll be sorry."

"No," I said. I almost laughed, but stopped myself. I wanted her to know how serious I was. "I definitely won't."

Outraged, Claire stomped away.

"Wow," one of the girls said. "You totally told her off." She looked impressed.

Her friends nodded.

"Yeah," I said, smiling now. "I guess I did."

35

When I got home that afternoon, I was surprised to see Dad sitting in the living room. He was almost never home before 6 p.m. He watched me as I came through the door.

I dropped my bag. "What's the matter?"

"Close the door and come inside," he said, his voice low and stony.

I did as he asked. Numbness began to spread from my middle to my limbs. I walked to the living room and sat across from him. "Is it Tara?"

"I got a very disturbing call today at the office," he said, ignoring my question.

I nodded.

"Mrs. Weinstein, the woman for whom you babysit."

Oh. I looked at the carpeted floor.

"She thinks you took something of theirs, something important to them."

I kept my eyes down, unable to look up. It was happening. I was getting caught. After all this time. I had thought about this moment often, but I had never imagined that I would be sitting across from Dad in the living room. I had never pictured any real-life details, actually. The idea of being found out had remained an abstraction.

"I denied it, of course. I couldn't imagine you doing something like that. But Mrs. Weinstein said there was no other explanation. The item had been there before they left, and when they returned, it was nowhere to be found. So I'd like to hear what you have to say, Lindsey."

I held still, unsure what to tell him.

"Is it true, Lindsey?"

I looked up at him finally, my eyes blurry with tears.

"My God," he said. He rubbed his face, that old familiar gesture. He stood and paced before me. My heart beat a mile a minute against my chest. "I defended you during that phone call, Lindsey. I said, 'Not Lindsey. She would never do anything like that.' " He stopped and looked at me. "Say something."

"I'm sorry," I blurted.

"That's it? You're sorry?"

I looked at my hands. They were shaking. I wanted to explain. I wanted him to understand. I steal because I'm empty. I'm angry. I'm alone. I steal because I want someone to notice me.

But Dad kept talking. "Do you have any idea of the position you've put me in?"

"This isn't about you," I said softly, but he didn't seem to hear.

"What would you have me do, Lindsey?" He was yelling now. "I have two daughters who are out of control."

"Why don't you try being a father," I said. If he wasn't

141

going to listen, I might as well say what I really wanted to say.

"What was that?"

I looked him straight in the eye. "Be a father," I said more loudly.

He watched me, his mouth slack. I had never spoken like this to him before. In my peripheral vision, I saw Tara standing at the entrance to the hallway. Wide mascaraed eyes watching.

I knew what I needed to say then.

"I'm the one who stole your credit card, Dad. Me. Not Tara. You would have known that if you ever paid attention to us. If you ever stopped worrying about your position long enough to see who we really are."

Dad shook his head. "Lindsey," he started, his voice calmer. "Listen."

"No," I said, not calm at all. "You listen to me. I steal things. I steal from you."

He shook his head again, as though he could make it not true. I stomped out of the living room, past Tara, and into my bedroom. I pulled the box out from under my bed and came back. Dad looked confused and disheveled, as always. And he watched as I dumped the contents of the box onto the floor. All the stolen things scattered. The pink ball from Mark's room rolled under the couch. I crouched down, searching for what I wanted.

And then I found it.

His wedding ring.

I plucked it up and threw it at him. I heard a noise come from Tara. The ring hit Dad's chest, then bounced back to the floor, where it rolled a few feet and stopped. Dad stared at it, speechless.

"Your ring!" I yelled. "Do you believe me now?"

Dad dropped to his knees. He picked up the ring. Something was happening, something coming over his face, but I wasn't ready to stop.

"You could have saved Mark if you had noticed," I said, my voice still loud. "He went to parties and drank, like any other fifteen-year-old. He wasn't some superstar on a fast track to medical school. He was just a kid, like me, who wanted his parents to see him for who he was."

I wiped hard at the tears with my sleeve.

Dad still crouched, bent over like an old man. When he looked up, there were tears in his eyes.

"Lindsey." His voice was a whisper.

I got up and walked quickly out of the living room, leaving the mess on the floor. I went past Tara, who stood dumbfounded in the hall, to my bedroom. I opened my desk drawer and riffled through the cards until I found the one I wanted. The one with the phone number. *Please call if you need anything at all.* I picked up the phone and dialed, sobs coming.

Diane Fanno picked up on the second ring.

"This is Lindsey," I said.

And, somehow, that was all I needed to say. It was as if she had been waiting for my phone call, waiting for the past two years.

"Go down to the lobby," she said. "I'll be right over."

36

Diane Fanno's eyes were big and brown and warm. In front of her now, the tearstains still fresh on my cheeks, I felt embarrassed.

"I'm so glad you called," she said.

I nodded.

"Should I take you to my house? Would that be too weird? We could go to a diner instead."

"No," I said. "Your house is fine."

She drove, and we stayed silent awhile. I watched out the window as we passed brick buildings and dark, leafless trees I knew by heart. Diane turned on the radio and classical music floated through the car. I took a deep breath, wondering what would happen next, now that I'd turned my life upside down. Dad had gone to his bedroom, and I hadn't seen him again before I'd left. That was the thing about being good—I'd known what to expect at each moment. I'd known what was expected of me. Now things were going to be different. There was no denying that.

Diane took a few turns, and soon we pulled into the driveway of a brick two-story house. The remains of a snowman stood in the front yard, two branches sticking out of its sides.

"My niece," Diane said, seeing me looking. "They were here over Christmas."

I didn't say anything. I didn't know yet how much I wanted to know about her life. Her life, which had kept going after that Halloween night, while ours had stopped.

Inside, the house was filled with Christmas decorations. Evergreen garlands and candles and red bows. A Christmas tree with white lights twinkled in a bay window. She urged me to sit and went to get us hot cider. I sat waiting, uncomfortable.

On a table next to the mossy-green couch, I saw a framed picture. It was the whole Fanno family: Diane, her husband, a girl, and Tim. Tim, who had been driving the night Mark died. I reached for the picture and studied it. I remembered Tim. He had dirty blond hair and a wide face like his mother. I had thought he was kind of cute. I could see that he had grown some, his jaw sharper, his expression more serious. Maybe Mark's death had been rough on him. I had never thought much about it before, but surely being the sole survivor must have changed him, forever taken something from him too.

"Tim has good memories of Mark," Diane said, placing the cider on the coffee table in front of me. I looked up, embarrassed to be holding the picture, but she didn't seem to mind. "We still talk about him often. I have memories of Mark too."

"Really?" I put the picture back on the table.

"He had a great sense of humor. He spent a lot of time here, making our whole family laugh."

I smiled, nodding, wanting more. I realized I had been

craving this. No one at home spoke about Mark, ever. Almost as if he hadn't existed. But he had. He had been right here in this house, making people laugh.

"Such a good-hearted boy too," she went on, taking a sip of her cider. "Tim used to give his sister, Emily, a hard time, but I would catch Mark letting her in on what they were doing sometimes."

I nodded again, remembering that about him. He was the one who taught Tara how to ride a bicycle because she wanted to come with us when we rode to the park. And when she fell the first time, he carried her all the way back home.

"I miss him," I said. "I miss him a lot."

Now Diane nodded, tears in her eyes. "I'm so sorry. I want you to know that. Tim is too. We're all terribly sorry. And I know being sorry isn't enough for what you've lost."

I looked down, my tears coming again too.

"I wish so much I could get Mark back for you. I wish I could start that night over again and be more adamant with Tim that he call us if he drank. But I can't. I can't get your brother back."

"I know," I said.

I glanced again at the picture, at Tim in his starched shirt and pants. I had never seen him dressed up. At our apartment, he'd always worn T-shirts and sweatshirts, a baseball cap with a curved brim.

"All I can do is try to make better what we have left."

I looked up at her, wondering if what had been left behind could be enough.

"I steal things," I told her.

146

She watched me. "Does it help?" she asked.

"No."

She waited.

"I stole from my family, my job, even kids at school."

She stayed silent, listening. No one had ever just listened before.

"I don't really know how to stop."

"Have you told anyone?" she asked.

"My dad knows now, but I don't think he understands."

"Maybe there's someone else you can tell."

I gripped my own hands. "Ms. Keller," I said. "I think I need to tell her the truth."

Diane smiled. "That sounds like a good idea."

I took a breath and looked back at the picture of her family. "Tim's lucky to have you," I said.

She reached out and hugged me, and I let my head rest against her shoulder. "Your family's lucky to have you, too."

37

After Diane dropped me off at home, I walked to the apartment door, my stomach tight and jumpy. I couldn't hide from this. I had mentioned most every off-limits topic in the book, and I didn't know what would happen when I walked through that door. For so long, I had wanted this: my world cracked open and changed. But now that it had happened, I was terrified. I used my key and stepped inside. All the things I had dumped were back in the box. It sat on the coffee table like some kind of center-piece. Someone was in the kitchen, opening and closing a cupboard. I walked slowly toward the sounds. It was Dad, and he was pouring pasta into a pot of boiling water. I didn't think I had seen him cook in years, maybe ever. Even weirder, Tara was sitting at the table, watching.

"Hungry?" Dad asked when he saw me. No stern voice, no anger toward me. Nothing.

I nodded, realizing that I was famished.

"Spaghetti and marinara okay?"

I nodded again, wondering what was happening.

"Tara," Dad said, "put out some plates, will you?"

Tara got up and went to the cupboard, where she

pulled down three plates. I watched, amazed. I looked back and forth between him and Tara. Something huge had shifted here. Tectonic plates had changed position. I looked at Dad, wanting to say something, but he met my eyes, a small smile on his face. A smile of apology. *You don't need to say anything,* his eyes said. I got it. He didn't want to talk. He didn't want to muck around in any heavy topics. Not wanting to talk about unpleasant things was par for the course for him, but at the moment, that didn't seem so bad. I could forgive him because whether we talked or not, everything was different now. I was different.

At dinner, we were all quiet. I pushed my fork around my plate, trying to get the words right. Finally, I looked right at Dad.

"I need you to help me," I said.

"Lindsey," Dad started, but I didn't want him to say the wrong thing.

"I have a problem with stealing and I need to see someone about it."

Dad cleared his throat. Tara looked from me to him, then back to me again.

"Do you hear her?" she said. "She said she needs help."

"I heard her," he said.

The phone rang, but for once Tara didn't jump to get it. She sat there with me, waiting.

"I'll talk to a colleague tomorrow."

I let out my breath.

Tara stuffed a piece of bread in her mouth. "Tell him our family's full of lunatics."

"Tara," Dad warned.

"Oh, come on," Tara said. "She threw your old wedding ring at you."

I met her eye and we both started giggling. It was sort of funny, remembering it now.

Dad looked at us, and we laughed harder. Finally, his face broke into a smile, a chuckle, and then he was laughing too.

38

Ms. Keller smiled as I stepped into her office. She looked genuinely happy to see me, which made what I was going to say ten times harder. I sat in the chair across from her desk. I crossed my legs one way, then the other. Finally, I just blurted it out.

"It was me."

She raised her eyebrows.

"I'm the one who stole from the lockers."

Her eyebrows stayed raised, but she didn't say anything, so I went on.

"When you gave me a new locker, I took the list of combinations." I squeezed my hands in my lap. "It was me."

Ms. Keller stared hard, taking this in.

"Oh, Lindsey," she said, the disappointment clear in her voice.

I felt like I might start crying. "I'm so sorry," I said.

"You understand I have to take action," Ms. Keller said.

I nodded.

"I need to think about what that action will be. Do you still have that list?"

I reached into my bag and handed her the locker combinations.

"I'll have to have all of these changed immediately," she said.

I didn't dare look at her. She couldn't trust that I hadn't made another copy. Why should she?

"I'm going to call your father and let him know I'm sending you home for the day. When you come in tomorrow, I'll tell you what I've decided."

I nodded.

"And, Lindsey?" I looked up at her. "I wish you had spoken to me. You could have confided in me, you know."

Tears stung my eyes. "I'm so sorry, Ms. Keller."

She just looked at me, the uselessness of my apology hovering in the air around us.

When I got home, I lay in bed and thought about change, how something so simple—like the loss of someone, or saying the unspeakable—can shake the world to its core, set off a spiral of events, so you can't turn back. How coming clean today would forever change who I might become. My ambassadorship would be gone. My school record was permanently tarnished. Johns Hopkins and medical school were out of the question. Suddenly the whole rest of my life lay unknown before me. This was new. I didn't know how I felt about it.

All the uncertainty felt frightening and invigorating at the same time.

Meanwhile, I had to finish what I had started.

I rolled over and reached beneath the bed, finding the box full of stolen items. I dug out the cuff links and placed them on my desk. I found a padded envelope and wrote the Weinsteins' address on the front. I dropped in the cuff links and wrote a quick note: "I know 'sorry' is not good enough, but I hope someday you'll forgive me."

I could give back the cuff links. I could bring back to school all the things I had taken from lockers. I could work off the money I had taken from Dad. I could even carry back to the stores all those little things I had stolen, still wrapped in their packaging. But there was more I couldn't give back. I couldn't give back to Ms. Keller or the Weinsteins their confidence in me. I couldn't protect Dad from the fact that I needed help. I couldn't return any of this more important stuff. Just as Diane knew she couldn't return Mark.

I sealed the envelope, thinking about how I wouldn't see Laird and Sol again. I wouldn't get to dance in their living room, Laird's laughter ringing in my ears.

But sending the cuff links, along with an apology, I could do.

Next I packaged the diamond earrings to send off to my mother.

39

The next day, Ms. Keller let me know her decision. I would return the items to each person and apologize, and I would serve detention each morning before school. As I knew she would, she took away my ambassadorship.

"I could have been much harder on you," she warned. "I could have turned you in to the police. I easily could have expelled you."

"I realize that," I said. "Thank you."

"And, quite frankly," she said, "I wanted to give you the benefit of the doubt. You've been a good student, Lindsey. One of my best. I had to assume there was something bigger going on here."

I nodded.

"Your father told me you would see a therapist soon."

I nodded again.

"That seems like a very good start."

At noon the following day, I sat inside the auditorium with the fifty or so other students trying out for *West Side Story*. Ms. Keller had agreed that my involvement in the play might be a good idea. She was being awfully kind, considering.

Kyle sat in the third row from the stage. I didn't know if he had heard about the stealing yet. Word was starting to spread. Missy was mad at me, but I knew she would come around in time. She was just disappointed, like everyone else.

Claire and Jo sat two rows behind Kyle. I could only imagine what Claire was saying about me now.

During Claire's audition, she belted out "I Feel Pretty." She went off-key a few times, but she wasn't too bad. When Mr. Zukowsky called my name, I climbed the stairs to the stage, told him I would sing "Somewhere," and waited for the music to start. I knew everyone's eyes were on me, including Kyle's, and I did my best to stare into the dimly lit rear of the auditorium, where no one sat.

At my cue, I began, allowing the song to take over my body, allowing myself to lift. I closed my eyes, feeling the music inside me. When it was over, I kept my eyes closed a moment. It had been a long time since I had sung like that. I had forgotten how it felt.

To my surprise, the room exploded with applause, and I opened my eyes.

"Wonderful," Mr. Zukowsky said when I turned to exit the stage. "Absolutely wonderful." As I descended the stairs, I met Kyle's eyes. His face was open, his eyes warm, like always.

I smiled.

Afterward, Kyle came up as I slid out of my row.

"You were amazing," he said.

"Thanks." So much had happened. My stealing. The thing with Claire. It was hard to know what to say.

"I'm sure you'll get Maria," he said. "You were meant for the part."

I shrugged. "We'll see."

We were silent, walking toward the doors.

"I guess you heard," I said.

"About you being the locker thief?" he asked.

I nodded.

"You're notorious, I'd say."

I laughed nervously. "I'm pretty screwed up, huh?"

He shrugged. "I think I know about being screwed up," he said. "I'm the one who threw a chair, remember?" He opened the door for me and I walked through. "You've got problems like everyone else. I wasn't falling for that best-sophomore-student thing anyway."

I laughed again. "You're really nice, you know," I said. "As much as you might think it's lame, you're nice anyway."

Now he was the one laughing. "I'm a nice person. How awful."

We stood outside the auditorium doors. Next period would be starting soon. A beat of silence passed.

"She really did force herself on me," he said.

"Whatever happened, it doesn't matter." I meant it. Considering everything I had done, it felt stupid to be mad at him over something so small.

"What's it going to take for you to believe that I like you?"

I pressed my lips together, my heart in my throat. I could feel my chest cave just looking at him.

"Let's start over," he said. "What do you say?"

I smiled. "I'd like that."

"I'm Kyle," he said, holding out his hand. "Misunderstood bad boy."

I laughed despite myself. "Lindsey." I took his hand, the warmth spreading into my arm. "Misunderstood good girl."

"I'm so glad to finally meet you."

I knew exactly what he meant.

Missy and Sam were already eating when I got to the cafeteria. I got my lunch—a cheese and avocado sandwich—and went to join them.

"Missy," I said when she ignored me. "You're going to have to talk to me eventually."

"All right. But I can't believe you did it. *You.*"

"I'm sorry, Miss. I understand if you can't be friends right now."

"Oh, shut up," she said. "I'm not going to drop you."

I smiled. She didn't smile back.

"But *you're* going to have to talk to *me* from now on. Understand? No more hiding."

"No more hiding," I said. "Promise."

"Please," Sam said. "I'm trying to eat my lunch here."

Missy glanced at him, annoyed. "I heard you told off Claire," she went on. She smiled now. "Perhaps there are things about this new Lindsey I can live with."

Claire entered the room. She scanned the tables, presumably looking for Jo or one of her other cronies. Rumor had it that she was back with Captain Lacrosse. I guessed that she had finally given up on Kyle. Or maybe it had finally sunk in that he wasn't interested in her. A boy I recognized from geometry approached her. He spoke to her, his hands in his pockets, shuffling his feet. Claire said something to him, and he walked away, looking broken. She scanned the room again, and this time her eyes caught mine. We held each other's gaze a moment. And then I smiled. Not a mean smile. A regular smile. A smile that meant I genuinely wished her well. She turned her head quickly, spotted someone, and strode off. I felt sorry for her.

Missy, who had been watching the whole thing, said, "You amaze me."

I shrugged. "I don't know why," I said. But I knew what she was getting at. I stood up and grabbed the tray that held my uneaten sandwich. "What kind of school serves avocado on a sandwich?"

Missy started to defend the avocado, but stopped. "Only ours," she said instead.

40

That weekend, Dad, Tara, and I stood together in Mark's room. Dad started by lifting a box and carrying it out to the living room. We were taking Mark's stuff to Goodwill. Not all of it, of course. I had made claim to his comics and high school essays, and Tara wanted a few of his old shirts. It was difficult to know what to hold on to—what made sense to keep around and what we needed to let go. This was Mark's life here—his entire life. There would be nothing more.

The day before, Mom had called about the earrings. She had received them, and she wanted to understand. I explained as best I could: the stealing, the way it had spiraled out of control, how I would be starting therapy. She had gone silent, overwhelmed with feeling, and for once I hadn't saved her from that. She had some growing to do too.

Now, in Mark's room, we stayed quiet except for the occasional comment: "Just a few more to go," "I'm right behind you." After we finished, Dad went down to the lobby to get a cart. When the last of the boxes was loaded, he nodded at Tara and me.

"I won't be long," he said. It was not a meaningful

statement, but I knew it was the best he could do. This was huge for him, cleaning out Mark's room, emptying the space of what was left of his only son. It was huge for all of us.

Tara and I stood in the carpeted space, looking at the blank walls and shelves, at the small bed that had once been the place our brother had slept.

"Weird," Tara said as she stood beside me.

"Yeah."

"Remember how he used to make us wait forever before he would let us in here?"

"That was just you," I said. I glanced at her and we smiled at each other.

"He was always nicer to you."

"Unless I was being mean to you. Then I was the one waiting out in the hall."

Tara smiled again. "Yeah," she said. "He was good like that."

We looked at each other a moment longer.

"Well," I said, "I guess we should dust and vacuum in here. Get it ready for whatever it's going to be next."

"Yeah," she said, turning to go. "Good luck with that."

I sneered at her, then got the vacuum from the hall closet. As I went to plug it in, I saw a small piece of paper lodged between the bed and the wall. I went down on my hands and knees to get it. On the paper was a smiley face, drawn in pencil. I turned it over, but there was nothing on the other side. I didn't know what it meant, if anything. But I could almost see Mark in my mind—a vision I was both afraid to have and afraid to lose, afraid I wouldn't have someday, time having erased the real-life, fleshy memory of him—my awareness of the way he must have looked when he drew that face, his smirk, the lightness that sat beneath it. He brought that lightness into our family. And now we were struggling to find a way to be happy without it. Sometimes missing him felt like a bottomless ache, like something I would never be free of. But I didn't want to stop missing Mark. And that knowledge made the ache bearable.

I got up and went to Tara's bedroom. The door was open.

"Look what I found," I said.

She came over and examined the smiley face.

"You can keep it," I said.

"Really?"

I nodded. She took it, holding it in her hands like a fragile thing.

"Thanks," she said.

Two days later, I came home to find the smiley face behind a glass frame, hung in the hallway for all of us to see.

41

Mr. Zukowsky walked through the crowd of kids waiting, unlocked the glass door, tacked up the paper, and locked the door again. My heart stuck in my throat as I approached, and I tried to calm myself. I really did want this, more than I had realized. Kyle came up beside me.

"The moment of truth," he said.

"I don't know if I can look."

"Come on," he said. He put an arm around my shoulders and led me into the crowd. My heart was beating like crazy. Claire stood near the front, Jo beside her.

"Anita is a great part," Jo was saying. "Better than Maria."

Claire watched me approach, looking unconvinced.

The parts were listed with the students' names beside them. I scanned from the bottom until my eyes rested on "Maria." And then my name.

My name. I had gotten the part of Maria.

I screamed, unable to control myself, and Kyle, his arm still around me, laughed. He leaned down to hug me, and before I knew what I was doing, I grabbed his face with my hands and pulled his mouth to mine. I stepped back, surprised at myself, but he put a hand behind my head and kissed me again. I knew everyone was watching. Including Claire. And I knew this was so unlike me.

Lindsey, the good girl.

Best sophomore student.

But I didn't care. I didn't care one bit. Because it didn't matter anymore what people expected from me. All that mattered was following my heart. So I kissed Kyle back, doing exactly that.

ACKNOWLEDGMENTS

I am grateful to Ethan Ellenberg, my agent, and Françoise Bui, editor extraordinaire, for seeing the good in this book. Thanks, as well, to Jenny Golub, who did the copyediting. Terri Brooks-Hernandez, my dear friend and recovering good girl, gave me the idea to write a book about stealing. The fly ladies of the Creative Children's Writers' Group—Laura, Lisa, Cheryl, Edna, Trish, Shelly, and Tia—saw an early draft of the first few chapters and offered useful critiques. I am always immensely thankful for Rebecca Grabill's insight. This time she helped me see what I needed to see, just when I was about to scrap the entire manuscript.

Thank you to Michael, classic good boy, who has to endure a cluttered house and preoccupied, distracted wife whenever I'm working on a book, which is pretty much all the time, and who has to keep a straight face when I tell him I *have* to watch *The O.C.* or *Gossip Girl*, or whatever teen drama is airing that night, because it's important research for my work. Finally, endless gratitude for my lovely, squishy, sweet-smelling little boys, who I hope will know they don't have to be good for anyone, and who can have whatever they want in their lives.

Kerry Cohen Hoffmann is the author of *Easy*, an ALA-YALSA Quick Pick and a finalist for the Oregon Book Award. She has worked as a psychotherapist, specializing in teen girls, and as a writing and literature teacher. Kerry lives in Portland, Oregon, with her husband and two sons. Learn more at www.kerrycohenhoffmann.com.